BRIDE UNTIL THE BORDER

A DARK MAFIA ROMANCE - NEVER BEEN CAUGHT 3

IVY WONDER

CONTENTS

Sign Up to Receive Free Books	1
Synopsis	3
Prologue	5
1. Chapter 1	15
2. Chapter 2	21
3. Chapter 3	31
4. Chapter 4	40
5. Chapter 5	45
6. Chapter 6	54
Intermission	61
7. Chapter 7	66
8. Chapter 8	74
9. Chapter 9	79
10. Chapter 10	84
11. Chapter 11	92
12. Chapter 12	101
13. Chapter 13	106
14. Chapter 14	110
Epilogue	113
Sign Up to Receive Free Books	117

Made in "The United States" by:

Ivy Wonder

© Copyright 2020 – Ivy Wonder

ISBN: 978-1-64808-112-5

ALL RIGHTS RESERVED. No part of this publication may be reproduced or transmitted in any form whatsoever, electronic, or mechanical, including photocopying, recording, or by any informational storage or retrieval system without express written, dated and signed permission from the author

❦ Created with Vellum

SIGN UP TO RECEIVE FREE BOOKS

Sign Up to Receive Free E-Books and Audiobook Codes.

Would you like to read **Savage Hearts** and **other romance books** for **free**?

You can sign up to receive free e-books and audiobooks by typing this link into your browser:

https://ivywondersauthor.com/ivy-wonders-author

SYNOPSIS

An abused woman and her daughter are freed from their terrible situation when an assassin takes out her monster husband. But now the assassin needs to get across the border—and he's using the woman and her daughter as camouflage. It's a race against time for the strange instant family as they try to get to Mexico before the authorities chase them down. Meanwhile, her playing the killer's fake wife has kindled some very real passion between them...

Blurb

My boss sent me to cancel an accountant who was skimming off the top.
He forgot to mention there's a kid.
And that the wife's a knockout.
I'm not about to disappear them, too.
Because of this, I've got to get over the border without backup.

They're looking for a man alone.
Not a man with a wife and young daughter.
The two of them are my ticket over the border now.
The family's fake ... but the attraction to my new "wife" isn't.

PROLOGUE

arolyn

DATE: February 2, 2019
   Location: Las Vegas, Nevada
   Subject: Brian Stone
   Criminal Record: Juvenile files sealed. Known associate of and presumed operative for the Las Vegas-based Cohen crime family. Suspected in the murders of five men connected to the Los Angeles-based Dragna/Milano crime family during their takeover war against the Cohen family between June and September 2017. Suspected in three additional murders: local methamphetamine dealer Kellan Keating in 2015, Cohen family-connected casino owner David Lutz in November 2017, and known Russian mob enforcer Vladimir Rostov in May 2018.
   Suspect is a former Navy SEAL who was dishonorably discharged when he became a suspect in Keating's death. He has never been connected to any of the murders except for hearsay;

there are no direct witnesses nor evidence. Informants in the area indicate that he has recently returned to the United States after an extended absence and is again living, and presumably working for the Cohens, in Las Vegas.

Stone has contacts in Baja California from his old outfit who are still loyal to him. It is presumed that he spent the last eight months in that area. His activities at that time are unknown. His return to the area likely indicates that the Cohens have called on him to eliminate another target.

"So who's the lucky guy?" *At least with my last suspect, I knew who his target was. Now, I have to butter up the Las Vegas cops to get help checking into new murders and hope that some of them aren't in the mob's pocket.*

I take a look at the file I was sent on Stone and shake my head. Yet another ridiculously hot, ridiculously hard to catch criminal, just like the last two. Those, I had actually caught— only to give them up out of a mix of sympathy and the chance to catch even bigger criminals.

The last one ended well. Instead of one mob hitter with thin evidence against him, I got seven mob hitters with extensive records. Now I was the flavor of the month here at headquarters —for the two seconds I got to spend in my home office, anyway.

Now I stare at Brian's photo and frown. The guy looks like a blond Clark Kent. Big, beefy, honest-faced, square-jawed, confident dark blue eyes steadily staring at the camera. His hair is short and spiky and the color of wheat. He's six-foot-four, well-sculpted, and flashing a movie-star smile. One of the surveillance photos is full-length; my eyes fix on the tight mounds of his muscular ass in well-worn jeans. I roll my eyes when I catch myself.

Ugh. I need to get laid, and soon. Either Daniels' list deliberately tortures me with the hottest men I have ever seen, or my thirst is making every man I run across look better. I can't even open the fifth file at all, or I'll end up staring at my last target's photo again instead of working.

And I'm still here to work. *Come on, Carolyn.*

I push back from my desk, rubbing the bridge of my nose. Between the red-eye flight into Vegas and the eye strain from typing reports, my head is pounding.

I walk over to the window of my fifth-story hotel room and stare out at a wet night gleaming with neon. My faint reflection is just an outline except for my pale blouse and platinum blonde braid. I look outside, deliberately focusing my tired eyes on distant things to rest them.

Far below, the streets still teem with people at four in the morning. The rumble of the city is relentless on the other side of the glass. I may have to wear earplugs to sleep; after weeks spent in tiny New York and Massachusetts towns, I've gotten too used to quiet.

At least I've finally left the snow and cold behind. Outside, it's a balmy sixty degrees even in the early-morning rain. I sat out a blizzard in the Berkshires just under two weeks ago and spent my last weekend in New York hunkered next to my heater while killer windchill howled through the streets. This, I could get used to.

And that's not even the end of the good news.

Assistant Director Daniels, my asshole boss, is off my back for a few days. I don't know all the details, but apparently, I'm not the only one that idiot decided to chase while his wife was beating breast cancer. Somebody dropped surveillance-tape footage into our section director's email box showing him harassing his secretary, and now Daniels has to go face a lot of questions.

I almost wish I was there to watch him squirm.

Daniels can't blame me for his current predicament, at least. I haven't even been in town. He's had me running my ass off up and down the East Coast and into Canada for weeks now. I only managed enough time back at my apartment to change the clothes in my suitcase. But I'm starting to wonder if I know who's responsible.

Prometheus.

While investigating Daniels' laundry list of unapprehended suspects, I managed to pick up a benevolent hacker ally. From the moment that list of five criminals dropped into my inbox, I started getting messages.

Texts from burner phones. Emails from untraceable accounts. Even a physical message during my last stakeout, elegantly written and delivered with a drink and dessert.

Whoever he is, he knows an awful lot about these cases, and about me and my travels. I sometimes worry about his level of access ... except that he's never been anything but helpful. He may have saved a few lives with his warnings—possibly even mine.

Now, I'm honestly wondering if he's my only chance of tracking down Brian Stone in a timely manner. Too much sniffing around in a heavily mob-controlled city—a city that the Cohens founded, for pity's sake—and I'll be inviting all kinds of trouble. I'm a lone FBI agent, the branch office here isn't offering much in the way of backup, and my boss is ... busy.

I'm exhausted, but I'm tempted to go out walking in this downpour. Eat a cheap casino steak, grab a brandy, then sleep on a full stomach after stretching my legs. It's too late for anyone to return my calls. Though Prometheus doesn't seem to sleep, so he's an exception.

Ironic that, once again, the outlaw hacker is more reliable than the Bureau.

Okay. One quick email, and then off I go to eat a nice chunk of cow and feel warm rain on my face.

I sit back at my desk and check my inbox—then sit there

blinking. The anonymous account he's using has already messaged me.

How was your flight? Too bad that the weather in Las Vegas is so dreary right now. I've left you a gift at the front desk, by the way. I hope that you like it.

Well shit. I've demanded more than once to know how he does this kind of thing, but he simply tells me that a magician never gives up his secrets. Infuriating ... and yet, he's sometimes the only one who really seems to be on my side. I type a reply while wondering how my life in the FBI has gotten so weird so fast.

Thank you. My flight was uneventful. I need to ask you about Brian Stone, alleged assassin for the Cohens in Las Vegas. I'm not sure why you're watching me so closely.

A minute later the reply comes.

Brian Stone wants out of the business. We have some associates in common and that rumor has been following him for at least half a year. I'm certain that he left the States temporarily in order to prepare for a more permanent escape offshore.

"Okay, well, that's something, but I'm not sure how to use it." Not sure yet, anyway. And yet ... it's a very familiar theme.

The first two men on Daniels' list wanted help getting away from crime families as well. The first one pissed off the first non-Genovese to sit as Don in New York City in decades. The other was tired of working for the Sixth Family up in Montreal. Now Brian wants to get away from the Cohens.

Daniels told me that the things these five men have in common are their extensive criminal non-records: crimes they were implicated in but could not be arrested on because of the lack of substantial evidence. In each case, he ordered me to track them down and bring them in for questioning in the hopes that they would either crack or ...

Or what? I haven't seriously questioned his motives for assigning me to these lukewarm, low-potential-close-rate cases, and I'm not sure why. I hastily type my reply.

Do you know who his new target for the Cohens is? The one he returned to the States for, I mean.

Another pause, this one shorter.

One moment.

I have to fight not to grind my teeth. My mind is racing.

So far, three out of three of the suspects have been trying to get out of bad situations involving the mob. The first one may have been by accident, but even he ended up linked to someone else escaping from the mob. Not that Daniels could have anticipated that ... unless he knows something I don't.

Which is likely. Agents get used by superiors with agendas all the time, and I'm new compared to everyone else in my office. And Daniels is a proven piece of shit who hates women who won't sleep with him. So what is he using me for?

I've got a list of criminals who don't want to be criminals anymore and who are connected with, or have dirt on, dangerous, highly sought-after crime families. Is he hoping these men will all turn state's evidence and that he can then take credit for the arrests they help us make?

My laptop beeps again. I open the email.

With the lack of current conflict between the Cohens and other crime families, I suspect an internal matter. There are six individuals that I know of who currently work for the Cohens who are no longer in their good books. I will forward you their information later this morning.

Relief rushes through me. I don't know how I would keep pulling hat tricks on these cases without this guy. But it still makes me wonder why the hell he is helping me in the first place.

I'm being screwed over and used by an assistant director of

the FBI and helped by an outlaw. I keep running into criminals who are more sympathetic than some of my coworkers. What the hell is going on?

I've always lived by strong principles. I've always used them, and my drive to make the world a better place, as my source of hope. They got me through Quantico. I don't know if they will get me through this.

I'm about to thank him when he sends a follow-up. I go still as I read it, my heartbeat in my ears.

When it comes to why I contacted you, the answers boil down to one thing: You interest me. And as for the particularly close attention right now, the situation is more urgent than usual. I'm afraid that you are more in need of help than you realize.

I have come to believe that your superior has deliberately given you a fool's errand of dead-end cases in order to discourage you into quitting. Now that the situation has escalated, he may intend to place you in harm's way. Have you heard from him lately?

A suspicion that has been nagging me lodges deeper into my head as I write my response. *He's a hacker. Building security at my office is accessible online. He could have hacked into our system.* I'm not sure whether I'm more comforted or worried.

Daniels is in trouble. Was it you, then? The footage sent to his superior?

I wait for five solid minutes for his reply, drinking hotel-room coffee and pacing, listening for the ding from my laptop to tell me that his reply has arrived. When his answer comes, I don't know whether to feel better or worse about it.

He needs to be kept busy for a few days while you are in Cohen territory. My influence there is limited. As I mentioned, I have evidence that he was going to escalate his revenge campaign against you.

I will give you more details once I have enough for you to act on. It would help if you would give me the reason for his peculiar vendetta.

I laugh sadly as I type my reply. There's no way of knowing how much of what he's telling me is crap, but he's provided nothing but solid leads so far. Daniels has always seemed to be out to get me—I just didn't know before now that it went this far beyond office politics.

I'm surprised you don't already know. Same as with the secretary and a bunch of other women. His wife got breast cancer, and he decided that the women working under him should fill in for her in the sex department. I hope she leaves him over this.

This time, the silence between replies is even longer. I go back to the window, yawning and waiting for all the caffeine and sugar from the coffee to hit my system. When my laptop beeps, the one-line reply surprises me.

And he did this to you as well? Does his wife know?

He almost seems angry. Why does this stranger give so much of a damn about me?

I close my eyes, trying to form an image of Prometheus in my mind. Brilliant, deeply interested in justice, totally disinterested in what's legal ... and somehow, for some reason, interested in me.

What are you going to do, Prometheus?

His reply is curt.

Kindly answer the question.

I take a deep breath. I'm standing at the edge of a cliff: one step forward will change my life forever. Certainly, it's going to change Daniels' life, because I'm sure that Prometheus is about to act on whatever I tell him.

If she hasn't filed for divorce yet, then no. She has no idea.

I think I need something stronger than coffee now. It feels like

I've just pulled the trigger on Daniels. But if even half of what Prometheus is saying is true—hell, even if it's all a lie—then Daniels deserves his wife's wrath and worse.

Then it is time to change that. Thank you for your cooperation. You will quickly find Assistant Director Daniels has been replaced or at least put on notice. By the Bureau, I mean. His wife may kill him.

Enjoy your gift, Carolyn.

"Thanks," I mutter, closing my laptop. I already know he's not going to reply again tonight. And I'm curious about that gift he's left me. I will probably be waiting for several hours to receive his list of Brian Stone's potential targets, so there's no problem in leaving my desk to take a little time for myself.

But the whole time I'm changing out of my winter clothes into jeans and windbreaker, I'm thinking about three men: Derek Daniels, Prometheus, and Brian Stone. Whatever Stone's reasons are for wanting to leave the mob, I'm willing to bet that he'll have valuable leads to trade in return for help getting out. If Daniels thinks he's the one who's going to get credit for those leads, he's in for a big surprise. And if he thinks he can set me up ... he's in for an even bigger one.

1
CHAPTER 1

Brian

"I can't believe you bought a damn island, man!" Jamie's cheerful voice over the hands-free speaker has a slight rasp to it; he's been smoking cigars behind his wife's back again. "What are you gonna do with it? Hang out on the beach and work on your tan?"

"Sunburn, Jamie. I'm a blond." He laughs and I chuckle as I drive my stolen van through a deep rain puddle. Water fans up on either side of my windows and then splashes down behind me. "Damn, this road is a piece of crap."

"Where the hell are you, anyway? It's gotta be four in the morning over there!"

"Running errands, man. My house has been shuttered for eight months. Nothing in the fridge."

My to-do list for tonight: drive out to southeast Las Vegas.

Kill an accountant who screwed the boss out of ten million. Buy milk.

"I get it. So can we borrow your boat for the weekend?" He sounds as eager as a kid. Jamie loves to fish: pargo, marlin, tuna —whatever he can catch and grill.

"Look, if you keep my boat safe and have it gassed up and geared up when I return, you can use it as much as you want. Seriously."

I keep my voice casual as I drive up the back road of the nature preserve just east of South Summerlin. My target's sprawling six-bedroom home backs up onto the preserve, providing a low, scrub-dotted hill that overlooks his fenced yard. The perfect spot for me to set up ... if this fucking rain thins out.

Otherwise, I'll have to go onto the property and take care of this up close. I hope not. But I'm gonna get soaked no matter what I do.

"Rain's getting thick over here, brother. Gonna have to hang up for now." I need to focus on getting the damn job done. Jamie doesn't know all the details of what I do, and it's better that he doesn't. We're both mercenaries, but I'm on permanent retainer to a crime family that likes its privacy.

The last thing I want to do is get my buddy in trouble with them.

"All right. But enough with running errands in that mess. Go home and get some damn sleep!" Jamie hangs up; I shut off the speaker and put all my attention on the dark road ahead.

This is the last job. Just get through it and get that last payday. Then you can retire from making widows to go where the Cohens can't reach you and where Jamie can come to visit all the time.

Jamie Chang wasn't kicked out of the SEALs like me. He took a bullet in an Iraqi operation and got his honorable discharge. All it cost him was a limp that gets gentler by the year.

He lives with his wife's family down in Baja—fixes boats

during the week and sails them on the weekends. Jamie's good people: loyal friend, loves his family, friendly with his neighbors. His life's uncomplicated and kind, give or take tight finances and the odd bad fishing day or sick kid.

Mine? Not so much. In the end, though, I can't really blame anyone but myself for that. Myself, and bad luck, and an offer I couldn't refuse.

I'll carry out this hit, send the proof to the boss, collect my money, and leave the goddamned country. And then I won't be doing anything with my life that I have to hide from my best friend.

He knows about the meth dealer that I shot, and he knows why. He doesn't know that the Cohens came and offered to make the murder charges go away if I came to work for them. It was that or prison; I took them up on their offer, and sometimes wonder if I should have gone the other way.

But prison would have made a murderer out of me, too, just to survive, and at least this way, I was free and getting paid. But after ten years ... it's just not worth it anymore. Even though none of the people I'm sent are innocent, their families are, and they end up losing a loved one.

Besides, sometimes it's dangerous. That guy Rostov ... half the reason for my extended vacation was healing up from all the knife scars he left on me. That crazy bastard took six bullets to mid-body and still had to take a knife through the throat before he would stop trying to kill me.

But it was him or me—or more importantly, me and the Don's thirteen-year-old granddaughter. Because the Russians wanted to break the old man's heart before Rostov killed him. But no damned way was that kid—any kid—going to die on my watch.

I might be the only guy who stumbled into being a mob

hitter *because* of his principles, not his lack of them. That time, it almost killed me.

And the old man barely gave me a thank-you after all that. The kid's actual parents showered me with cash the Don doesn't know about, but as usual, that prick just saw it as my job. Which is part of why I now can—and will—retire to a secret island paradise well outside of American borders.

Money's remarkably good at solving problems.

Thunder rumbles in the distance, and the wind blows sideways rain against my windows. I wouldn't even be out in this shit if the Don hadn't ordered that the job be done tonight. Sniping in the rain isn't easy and being on a bare hillside in a thunderstorm isn't smart.

All the more reason I'm eager to get the hell out of this job.

I make it to the right spot and park, waiting for the rain to stop coming down in sheets. I can plainly see the property's backyard with its pool and Jacuzzi, including a solid line of sight to their back door, but that doesn't help me much. In this weather, Toby Whitman's not likely to come outside where I can shoot him quick and clean.

Either I go in ... or I lure his ass out and put a bullet in him that way.

The problem with going in is that he's a married man. I don't like collateral damage, and I know the Cohens' "no witnesses" policy will lead to a dead, completely innocent wife if she's home. I'll have to be smart instead.

My disguise, which extends to the power company van I've been supplied, is a utility worker dealing with late-night outages. Waterproof jumpsuit, toolbox with a silenced .45 nestled inside. Hat to cover my hair.

In a storm like this, vans from the power company are ubiquitous. Nobody notices them—or remembers them if they do.

I wish I could have gone in full disguise, but aside from

changing hair and eye color and dressing differently, there's not much point. I'm not a good enough liar to make up some bullshit new identity for myself on the fly if someone questions me. So instead, I wear the uniform and drive the truck given to me, and follow my orders, just like I did in the military.

I've only ever killed one person because I wanted to ... and even then, it wasn't so much a desire as a need. It wasn't worth it; I've paid for that choice ever since. But everything before or after that was different. Tonight is different.

Killing mobsters is like killing the enemy on the battlefield. The bastards know what happens in the underworld. You step the wrong direction, you die.

This guy Toby stepped the wrong direction. And then he kept stepping. Jacob, my handler, showed me the goddamn books this guy skimmed from for ten years. Millions of dollars.

I don't know why he thought that shit would work—how he figured nobody would notice. He was pretty subtle the first few years: a thousand here, a couple hundred there, nothing the boss would really miss. But then he got greedy. He got more obvious. Bigger numbers. More frequent thefts.

There's only so much bullshit you can get away with around here before you pay for it. Toby was a good accountant. He just made two mistakes—he thought he could scam the Cohens, and he did it so badly, he got caught.

Now I'm out in the rain taking care of the matter. And for that, I'd like to kick Toby's ass before the bullet. But I have to keep discretion in mind.

The wind's gusting across the hillside, the rain's slamming against the grass hard enough to flatten it, and as I stare down the hill at Toby's backyard, it becomes clear that sniping isn't going to do the job tonight. I'll have to get closer.

" ... fuck." Why is the boss so eager to get this done tonight?

It's easy to give a kill-order when you're not the one crawling through the chaparral in a damn monsoon to get it done.

I peer through the rain at the back door, trying to figure out how I can get that asshole outside and away from his wife, so I can shoot him and go home. I could make noises out here—make him think it's an animal or a neighbor kid. But then he might call the cops before coming outside.

Then my gaze falls on his satellite dish. It's one of those giant deluxe deals that could probably catch a broadcast from Mars—if it's pointed in the right direction. Point in the wrong one, and it stops picking up all those premium channels that he likely pays over two hundred a month for.

I smile slowly as a plan forms in my mind. I'll lure him out in this mess after all, using a handy little rich-guy problem. One that will probably drive him into such a froth, he'll never expect the ambush out here waiting for him.

CHAPTER 2

Ophelia

I HEAR a crash downstairs from my husband knocking something over in a fit of anger. I freeze. I'm hovering over my daughter's bed, having just soothed her back to sleep after another early-morning nightmare. The sound of Toby's rage makes me want to hide under it instead.

The storm's messing with the satellite reception for some reason, and that has Toby pissed off again. I can hear him pacing from room to room, his breath huffing, while I hold still in Molly's room and fearfully listen for his footsteps on the stairs. Once he comes up to me, I know what's going to happen.

Not in front of Molly. He won't dare.

But Toby makes excuses, and he escalates. Slowly, slowly, over years—each time coming out of it full of apologizes and promises to be better. Promises that always prove as empty as his supposed love for me.

The locket that my grandma got me? Shattered under his spiteful heel as he stomped it five times. Here's a shiny ring to make up for it. The glass he threw at me? Swept up and replaced. That broken jaw on my birthday? He'll never ever do it again.

I only stay for my kid, and because I'm scared of what he'll do to retaliate if I take her and run. Toby's bosses are dangerous men, and they absolutely will catch me and return me to him. Toby's bosses are the Cohens.

Nobody escapes the Cohens. And so, I can't escape Toby. All I can do is hope that he punches the wrong person during one of his temper tantrums or has a heart attack from all the rage.

It was nice at first to be with someone who always had money. It was nice not have to worry about that for the first time ever in my life. At the time, I was desperate, and he took advantage.

I came to Las Vegas with big stupid dreams and got slapped down by reality, like a million other girls. My waitressing job barely kept me in an apartment I shared with three people. My tries at being a showgirl went nowhere because I wouldn't fuck the guys doing the casting.

By the time Toby came along, acting kind and generous and treating me like a lady, being poor and scared in Las Vegas had already dulled my judgment. When he invited me to move in so I wouldn't have to struggle, I agreed. By the time I realized what a stupid mistake that was, Molly was already in my belly.

Toby's actually not bad with his daughter. He dotes on her. He's never violent around her.

Ironically, that makes it harder to believe him when he claims he just "loses control" with me. I know better; Toby's a small man with a small dick. He uses violence to keep me in line so he can feel big.

But at least he doesn't touch his daughter or do anything to me around her aside from yelling. He hasn't gone that far. So I linger in her bedroom, wondering how long that small, limited space will actually be safe from him.

Probably not long at all. He'll call me out if all else fails, and there are consequences if I don't promptly respond. In the end, it's all about control with him—control of me, as his property.

Mom was right about him. She did the bare minimum for me when I lived under her roof; she had wanted a boy and had no problems reminding me of that every time I annoyed her. Which was as easy as breathing too loudly.

But she told me the bald truth about Toby. I needed to hear it, and I didn't listen.

It doesn't matter how nice he is, Ophelia. That man will hurt you. And he's probably disappointing in bed.

I blink back tears. *Two for two, Mom. Not that I would ever admit that to you.*

Molly is my consolation prize for this terrible marriage, and I don't know how much longer I can keep her around him before she starts to suffer, too. I have to find a way out. One that won't end with me dead or in jail.

My baby needs me.

He's called the satellite company. I can hear his half of the conversation now as he paces around on the flagstone hallway floor, wingtips clicking.

"I'm *telling* you that I pay through the nose for the deluxe package every *single* month, and I *want* you to get a man down here to fix this *tonight*! You're not the only game in town, you know!" He starts huffing so loudly that it sounds like he's right next to me.

Shit. I sometimes wonder how he's kept from being shot by his own employers; he has so much trouble keeping his temper under control. He's raged us out of doctors' offices, gotten us blacklisted by repair places, even thrown a can of soup at a meter maid. That last one nearly had him arrested; I'm sure it was the Cohens who kept him out of jail.

"I want to speak to your manager now!" he yells, and then lets out a blue streak of swearing, probably in response to being put on hold.

How much longer until he kills me or attacks Molly? How many more scars do I have to wear on my skin and heart before this is over? I don't know what hurts worse: the fear, the despair, or the helpless rage.

Two months ago, after I returned from a stay in the hospital thanks to a "little fall" down our main staircase, I got up in the middle of the night, snuck downstairs, and came back with a filleting knife from our kitchen. I stood by his side of the bed, staring at his sleeping face, at the skinny neck just below it, weighing my options and the blade in my hand.

I could get in one good slash before he woke up, I figured, and if I didn't hit a blood vessel, he would get up and attack me, and I would never have a second chance. But it was almost worth the risk for the chance to be free.

The thing that made me hesitate was the idea that he might kill me, and then Molly would be alone with him.

In the end, I put the knife away and went to check on my baby daughter to remind myself that there are other ways.

I just haven't found anything that works yet.

"Fuck you, then, you damned grunt worker! You don't know anything!" He throws the phone down with an expensive-sounding crack, and his quick, light step gets quicker as he paces through the foyer and then back again.

My heart's pounding in my ears as I step out of Molly's room and shut the door softly, unwilling to hide in her space forever. That isn't right. The shouting might wake her up; she might see her mother get hit.

So, even knowing how it's going to end, I walk away, like a

mother tern dragging a wing to lure the fox away from her nest. I smooth the front of my demure white nightgown and hope that rough sex is all the bastard will demand this time.

"Ophelia!" The roar makes me jump. I don't know how that reedy little shit of a man manages to be so aggressively scary, but here we are again, my skin already starting to crawl in anticipation of pain.

I force myself past Molly's room, all the way to the head of the stairs. "Yes?" I keep my voice calm. *Never let him see you sweat.*

Toby glares up at me, his glasses and bald spot shining in the light from the foyer's gaudy crystal chandelier. Behind those blank circles, his small black eyes will be just as empty. He's in a dangerous mood, forgetting any pretense of love and decency.

But instead of stomping up the stairs, he points down the hall toward the back door. "Go out and check the fucking radar dish."

That's unexpected. But it doesn't involve bleeding, so I'm instantly onboard. "Okay, let me get my coat and shoes. Where's the flashlight?"

He turns purple in an instant, lurching toward the base of the stairs with his fists already up. "I said get your ass outside and check! Now!"

Frozen inside, I mechanically descend the stairs, eyes focused forward as he stares at me. I have to do what he wants, with no emotional reaction, or the beating will start.

I've had nightmares about having to cross a floor full of marbles in the dark with a vial of nitroglycerin in my hand. That's this same feeling. During dream time, I can scream and cry. Right now, I can do neither, or it will set him off.

Sometimes, calm-seeming obedience works, and he calms down himself and returns to his porn and his conversations with the shady fuckers he works with. Or he orders me upstairs and out of my clothes for a few minutes of uncomfortable fucking.

Either way, I have to rest for a while afterward, the same as if I were beaten—but without the pain and terror haunting me for days afterward.

Toby's stare bores holes in me as I walk past him, giving as wide a berth as I can afford. I know he wants me to fuck up somehow. Step the wrong way. Shed a tear. Give him an excuse.

But I'm getting good at this. I walk past, face blank, on the way to the back door, as my anger starts to melt away the terror. I don't so much as twitch as I follow orders. Here I am, going out in a sixty-degree rainstorm in my nightgown—but I still haven't given him the excuse he wants to start beating me.

He starts huffing again as I walk away from him, pissed off that I'm not pissing him off. His twisted principles won't let him lash out at me unless he can excuse it in his own head. That takes almost nothing—but as long as I give him the illusion of total control over me, his thirst for violence can't come out.

It's like a cross to a vampire—at least until he finds a way to rationalize breaking his own rules so that he can get his fists on me anyway. That's happened before, too. And that's why I'm starting to worry about my daughter.

I should have stabbed him. It's easy to hide a body out in this desert. And I already know how to get blood out of bedding.

"Hurry it up," he snarls. I put my hand on the door and brace myself, then open it and step out into the rain.

It's like being hit with a fire hose. I stagger under the weight of the wind-blown torrent, gasping and blinking. I'm soaked instantly, shivering, the sodden flannel sticking to me as I lurch across the yard toward the blurry, shadowed outline of the satellite dish.

I can already see something odd about it. The dish's angle is off from where it is usually. Did the wind do it?

It's the one part of the yard that the light doesn't reach; I move forward very cautiously, feet squishing into the muddy lawn. The wind shoves me sideways. Toby's yelling something at me from the doorway; I pretend I can't hear. Instead, I push on, determined to get this done and get the hell inside.

I stop short when I see the problem: the dish is turned completely around. Did the wind somehow manage to snap the bolts? Catch the dish like a sail and turn it?

"Damn it." I sigh, pulling the sodden fabric away from my thighs and moving forward into the shadows. I can feel Toby's eyes on me, like a piece of hot metal being held against my skin. *I would give anything to get myself and my baby away from you.*

But for now, I have to figure out if this mess can be fixed and the monster in the doorway mollified. I lean down to check the bolts holding the dish in place and find them loosened. Frowning, I straighten. Suddenly, a huge figure leans out from the shadows and grabs me.

My squeal of surprise is immediately muffled by a big gloved hand; the man pulls me backward into the darkness so fast that I freeze. "Be quiet," a deep voice says calmly in my ear. "I'm not here to hurt you."

Strangely, the man's grip on me is firm, but not rough; his hand covers my mouth, but his tone is reassuring. His big body behind and hovering over mine radiates heat and blocks the rain.

"Call for your husband," says the voice in my ear.

I freeze, mind racing. This man is here to kill Toby.

Is he from a rival crime family? Or did Toby finally screw up badly enough that the Cohens want him gone? Either way ... I know what happens when Toby comes over here. He's going to eat a bullet.

I may die, too, but ... opportunity knocks but once.

He removes his hand from my mouth. "You going to kill me when you're done?" I demand in a low voice.

"No. You didn't piss off the boss. But if you don't cooperate, I'm gonna have to knock you out."

"I have a six-year-old daughter inside," I warn him, and feel him stiffen slightly.

"You had better not be lying."

I realize the strangest thing about this moment isn't that there's a hitter behind me telling me to call my mob accountant husband across the lawn so he can be shot. The strangest thing about this is that the hitter's touch is gentler than my husband's.

"Toby!" I call out at the top of my lungs.

"What, bitch?" he roars in response. "I'm not coming out there!"

The man behind me unsnaps something, and I hear the rasp of a gun clearing leather. And suddenly the anger that has been simmering in me for years boils over. "I said I needed the flashlight for a reason, you bratty little shrimp-dick. Now grab it and get your hairy ass over here!"

The guy behind me startles slightly and then starts to shake, and I realize he's laughing silently. Guess he expected me to obey out of fear. But I have plenty of other reasons to cooperate with a hit on Toby.

"What?" Toby's voice cracks in a way that sends slivers of ice through my heart. But I know now that he's never going to lay hands on me again—and I'll never again get the chance to tell him what I really think. "What did you say to me?"

"You heard, you weak piece of shit! Make yourself useful for once in your life. Get the fucking flashlight and get over here!"

Holy shit. I just said that out loud. More than that—my voice was harsh with absolute disdain. After years of suffering under his fists, under his rules, with every aspect of my life controlled … it feels good to tell this prick off.

"When you come back in here, I'm going to kick your ass, whore!" he roars, his voice barely audible above the rising wind.

I wait until it dies down a bit, then call out even louder, "Come out here and do it then, you coward! Or are you scared that getting your hair wet will make your bald spot look bigger?"

His inarticulate growl of rage mixes with the click of the stranger's finger tightening on the trigger.

And then Toby loses control, stomping across the lawn, no longer caring about the rain or anything else. Hungry to beat me, to yank out my hair, to slam my face into the rim of the satellite dish. Eager to get started with what he's been working himself up to all night.

The man with an arm around me—his big, hard body against my back—stiffens slightly again and tightens his grip on me, though not painfully. Protectively. He turns aside, actually lifting me one-armed for a moment and setting himself between me and my charging husband.

He's a mob hitter! Who does that?

Toby's so blind with rage and thirsty for my blood that he doesn't notice the guy in the shadows until he almost runs into us. Then he notices the pistol pointed at his nose and skids to a stop, mouth dropping open in horror.

"This is for skimming off the top for ten years. And for being a piece of shit husband," the stranger adds. "You got anything for me to bring to the bosses besides your death photo?"

"I ... I ..." Toby stares between us as I stand mutely, bracing myself for the gunshot. "I didn't—"

"Ten million dollars, buddy. And you actually thought that nobody would notice." The stranger sounds almost amused, his voice chiding. "What did you think was gonna happen? Did you plan to scapegoat your wife for that, too?"

The edge in the stranger's voice fascinates me. But what fascinates me more is the pallor in Toby's face as the lightning throws bright light across the yard. My husband's eyes meet mine ... and then fill with impotent rage. "You sold me out—"

"No, she didn't." And then the thunder rolls. The gunshot stings my ears but still gets lost amid the sounds of the storm.

Toby grunts once, hand over his chest, his eyes enormous. He locks eyes with me and my heart splits in two: half already grieving the man I knew who was just an act to lure me in, and half relieved that the real Toby's finally gone. I remember the broken jaw, the replaced tooth, the miscarriage from being beaten in the belly ... and force a smile.

It's the last thing he sees before his eyes glaze over, and he falls backward into a heap on the lawn.

I let out a relieved sob, and the man lets me go. But he doesn't holster the gun. After a moment, I realize it and turn around nervously.

The gun's down at his side, but the shadowy figure is just standing there, looking at me. I catch sight of a utility jumpsuit and cap and a pair of denim-colored eyes that stare at me with surprising concern.

"Now what?" I say breathlessly, trying to ignore the death rattle behind me.

CHAPTER 3

Brian

I'M SUDDENLY DEALING with three unexpected factors all at once. Factor number one: the guy's wife saw the whole thing; she even helped me, and I doubt it was just because she was scared. From the way he was acting, Toby Whitman's been making her life hell.

Factor number two: they have a small daughter. Yet another reason for me to break the Cohens' "no witnesses" rule.

Factor number three: she's the most beautiful woman I've ever seen.

Soaked, exhausted, terrified, golden hair askew from its chignon, wide brown eyes full of fear ... this delicate-featured sylph is staring at me like she's as baffled as I am about how to proceed. Her husband is breathing his last and she looks ... relieved.

And I'm both shocked and glad.

"He was hurting you." I holster the gun. I'm not using it even if she runs away, screaming for the police. Her husband was my last kill. I'm done.

"Our whole relationship," she murmurs, gazing up at me. She relaxes a little more when I holster the .45. "You're from the Cohens."

"Formerly. This was my last job." I rub my chin as I look her over. "Let's get you inside and talk. I think we might be able to help each other out."

"If you do anything to hurt my child—" she starts, but I shake my head.

"I'm not a piece of shit like your husband. I want to make a deal, not cause more problems." I turn around and stare at the sprawled figure on the ground. "Go inside. Get changed. I'll take care of this."

I don't know why I trust her not to go to the police. Maybe she's figured out that she just helped lure her husband to his death, and that won't look good to the cops. Maybe she's too glad he's dead to give me much trouble. But when she nods and turns to head inside, I feel nothing but relief.

Off the guy goes into the body bag. He doesn't weigh much, even limp. I scoop him up over one shoulder, go back over the fence, and get him up and into the van. There's an open grave waiting for him out in the desert.

Luckily for me, I didn't have to dig it. Some other guy who's a touch lower on the boss's shit-list than Toby here got the duty. It's better than a bullet—but in this weather, not by much.

For a few seconds, I think about getting into the front seat of the van and just driving off. The police are mostly in the Cohens' pocket, and I know that I didn't get caught on CCTV. Toby's wife seems relieved that he's dead.

I want to move on and leave her alone to be a wealthy widow. She can simply tell everyone that her husband has disappeared.

Except ...

Except she might be just as bad a liar as I am. And even if I'm out of the country, that's trouble that could follow me. And ...

And if she talks to the police, if they break her, the Cohens will send someone next time who doesn't give a shit about shedding innocent blood.

"I gotta take her with me." It sounds ridiculous even as it comes out of my damn mouth. "Her and the kid. The only place they'll be safe is away."

That's crazy, though. If they're watching for me at the border, she'll be endangered all over again if she's with me.

Unless ...

Maybe I'm tired. Maybe it's the fact that I'm getting soaked. Maybe my judgment is slipping, because I'm on my way out of the whole goddamn business anyway.

Or maybe it's her. Unexpectedly.

Maybe it's those enormous brown eyes, now burned into my memory, staring at me like I was a goddamn hero. The last time someone looked at me like that, it was my neighbor's daughter. The one who I rescued from that fucking meth dealer.

I'm just glad that she doesn't have any idea that I was gunning for whoever came out to fix the damn satellite dish, and that I hadn't expected the lazy, abusive prick to send her out in her nightgown in his place. Good thing she doesn't know that a moment before I reached out to grab her, I was hurriedly returning my pistol to its holster. I hope she never learns that I came close to shooting her by mistake.

That's probably part of it—the guilt. I've killed exactly zero innocent people in my life. If they weren't armed, dangerous, and on my boss or the government's kill list, I wouldn't touch them. All except for that dealer—the one whose death ruined my life.

Coming close to killing that beautiful young mom rattled

me. She seems to think I'm a hero for freeing her and her daughter from whatever her husband was doing to them. Knowing how close I came to a fatal fuck-up, I want to be that hero for her now.

I close my eyes. *Do I go talk to her, or drive away and hope this doesn't fuck up or end her life?*

"I go talk to her." My own answering mutter rises over the rattle of the rain. I sigh, shaking my head. This is probably ill-advised, but it's also probably the right thing to do.

When I return to her yard, I hesitate, not sure whether I should knock or just walk inside. It seems a touch ridiculous to be so polite, but she's not a target. She's a woman I'm about to do a quick, and hopefully mutually beneficial, negotiation with.

I knock on the mullioned glass back door and wait politely under the awning for her to answer. Instead, what I get is a tiny girl in an enormous powder blue T-shirt, her straight chestnut-brown hair mussed from sleep. She comes toddling down the stairs, taking each one very carefully, her big brown eyes full of determination.

Oh. Uh. I stand there blinking. Unexpected scenario number two in this morning's job: itty-bitty adorable kid with insomnia. Yay.

I try to rearrange my expression into a pleasant smile as she walks up to the glass and considers me with a tiny soft-mouthed frown. "Hi there. Can you get your mom? You shouldn't open the door by yourself."

That's the kind of responsible grown-up stuff you're supposed to say to kids, right? It's been a while for me.

She frowns and reaches for the knob. "It's raining! You're gonna get cold!"

"No, no, you don't know me, honey. Don't open the door for strangers. Some of them aren't nice. Just wait for your mom." *Well, this is awkward.*

I don't know what her mom wants to tell her daughter about what happened and why her father is gone. I don't know if she's scared of her dad, if she loves her dad, or both. I have to let her mother take the lead on this one ... because I stepped out of my depth the moment the kidlet wandered up to the door.

"Mommy's crying in the shower. Come in and make me cocoa." She pouts rebelliously and starts twisting the knob. "It's cold and rainy! Don't be dumb!"

"Uhhhh ..." It's going to look really bad to this poor woman if she comes back from showering and I'm in her house with her kid in the same room. "It's okay, sweetie. I gotta let your mom decide. Those are the rules. If she lets me in, I'll make you cocoa."

Footsteps patter on the stairs. I look through the foyer to the grand staircase and see that soft-eyed blonde sylph coming down wrapped in a spa robe, hair in a towel. She looks worried and darts forward when she sees her daughter trying to let me in.

The girl looks up at her, pouting. "He's dumb. He won't come in unless you say it's okay! But it's all rainy and I want cocoa."

She relaxes slightly and looks up at me. I nod to her—and see her eyes widen slightly as she gets a look at me in good light.

I have to fight to keep my smile from turning into a grin as her gaze sweeps over me. There're a lot of women out there who like a big, built guy who knows how to be gentle. And my one encounter of Toby and their relationship has already told me that the man wasn't doing it for her in bed—or anywhere else.

"Oh did he? Well good. You know you're supposed to wait for me." She gently shoos her child away from the door and moves forward to open it. "Come in."

I make sure not to make any sudden moves as I walk into the house, but I do sweep the whole area with my gaze. This house has no cameras up anywhere that I can see. My guess is, Toby was a straight-up wife-beater and didn't want any cameras around to document his assaults.

"What's your name?" she asks in a faint voice. I look over and see her already slipping off her wedding ring and putting it in her robe pocket. I don't know if that's for my benefit, or because it's felt like a manacle during her marriage to that nasty little creep.

Probably the second, no matter how much my ego would like it to be the first.

"Brian. You?" I'm keeping my manner as calm and friendly as possible. The presence of the child demands lightness even in this crazy-heavy situation.

"Ophelia. This is Molly." She gives me a tiny smile despite the red eyes. "She's six."

I give the kid a smile. "Hi, Molly. Nice to meet you."

"Cocoa!" comes the squeaky demand, and Ophelia and I exchange awkward glances.

"Uh yeah, sure." I let Ophelia—lovely name for a lovely girl—lead us into the kitchen. She glances at me nervously a few times, and I struggle to keep my eyes off the gorgeous curves of her ass as they push out the white terrycloth.

"Do you want something stronger than cocoa?" she asks me as she fishes through the cabinets, and I pull milk out of the fridge. She is keeping herself calm, acting normal, probably for the sake of her kid. But her eyes are still red, and I know she's having a hard time.

"Peppermint schnapps, if you've got it." I want to dive into telling her that I'm sorry and promising I'll help make sure she doesn't see any blowback from this. But right now, reassuring the little one that nothing weird or scary is going on must be the top priority. You get on a woman's bad side fast if you scare her kid.

"I just have Kahlua and whiskey." She looks at me over her

shoulder and I notice the fading bruise on her cheekbone. The shower must have washed off the makeup covering it. She really is used to taking a punch. This is just ... sick.

"Actually, Kahlua sounds good. Thanks." I give her a smile, and she looks away shyly. *Stop it, Brian. Now is not the time to flirt even if she's as grateful as she seems about having her husband dead. She was still crying in the shower. She's too vulnerable for me to push into anything. It wouldn't be right.*

"Okay." She sets the bottle on the counter nearby and keeps digging as I get the milk simmering.

"So, do you want your cocoa with lots of marshmallows or super-duper lots of marshmallows?" I ask Molly as a bag of mini-marshmallows gets set on the counter near me. I'm stirring chocolate shavings from a zip-top bag into the milk.

"Super-duper lots!" the kid insists, beaming up at me with enormous eyes that look so much like her mom's.

What the heck is even going on here? I think as her mother silently lines up three mugs on the counter. "Is Mom okay with super-duper lots?" I check, since I'm not sure about letting the kid bounce off the walls on a sugar high in the predawn hours. My own parents wouldn't have given a shit, but I know real ones do.

"It's fine. She's just going to be up at this rate. You want to watch your Miyazaki movies after cocoa, honey? We need to do some boring grown-up talk."

"*Spirited Away!*" Molly squeaks, seeming delighted that nobody's telling her to get her butt to bed. I chuckle and shake my head, continuing to stir.

Funny thing, though. She hasn't once asked where her dad is.

Once Molly is set up in the TV room with the door closed, her movie on, and cocoa that's a quarter marshmallow in her hands, Ophelia turns to me with her hands clasped in front of her. "Let's go upstairs."

I try to ignore my dick's response to an invitation that has nothing to do with sex, and simply nod, following her back to the stairway and up the stairs.

"Can you tell me the whole story of why my husband is dead now?" she asks in her low, gentle voice.

"I was told he skimmed ten million over the course of the last decade. He was paid well, but he couldn't have afforded this place without stealing from someone. He chose the Cohens." I sip my drink as I follow her, not elaborating.

"That sounds like a terrible idea." She leads me into what turns out to be a small office. From the pretty, comfortable chairs to the floral artwork on the walls, I suspect it's hers. "Please have a seat. I um ... I don't know what more to ask about it."

I settle into one of the overstuffed recliners. She curls up on the couch across from me, sipping her drink. "It's pretty open and shut. He was embezzling, he got caught, he denied everything. That earned him the bullet."

I'm trying to keep my voice gentle, but she stiffens slightly. I wait until she's fortified herself with another swallow. She doesn't speak again, so I go on.

"The bosses ... my now ex-bosses ... don't like witnesses, and they don't like loose ends. That's why I tried to lure him out of the house. If things had gone as planned, well, you wouldn't even have seen me. He would have just vanished out of your backyard."

"I see." She presses her lips together and gazes into my eyes. "So the Cohens will want me dead, then. And my child." Tears sparkle in her lower lashes, and my heart sinks.

"If they find out you saw anything, yes. They'll send someone who doesn't have the ethics that I do, and he'll finish the job." I rub a hand through my hair, looking away from her. "I'm sorry."

"But you didn't come back here for that. So, what—a warning to get out of town?" Her voice shakes.

"More like an invitation. A way for *all of us* to get away from the Cohens for good." When she blinks in surprise, and hope shines faintly in her eyes, I smile for real.

CHAPTER 4

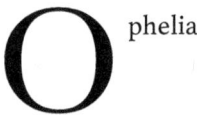

THE MOST PRIMALLY ATTRACTIVE man I have ever seen in the flesh is sipping Kahlua-spiked cocoa with me in my office not half an hour after gunning down my husband with my help. I roll this fact over and over in my mind as he calmly explains our current predicament—and his proposed solution.

"So, we find what's left of the stolen millions and anything else we can take with us, you pack bags for yourself and the kid, and we take off for Los Angeles. We get a fresh car and some tourist clothes, then head for Baja." He lifts his eyebrows slightly. "How's your Spanish?"

"Uh ... well..." I smile sheepishly. "My neighbor's been teaching me bits. But I know my accent probably hurts her ears, and I'm likely talking gibberish half the time." Maria's going to wonder what the hell happened if I disappear suddenly.

I'll have to send her an email with something about getting

away from Toby and not being able to talk about where I am right now. She's been encouraging me to go to a shelter with Molly. I'll tell her I'm okay, and then just let her assume that a shelter is where I've gone.

Brian snorts and looks down into his mug. That thin little smile of his charms me more than a grin would. A grin from a guy I know can kill would just make me nervous. "It's all right. I learned from a native, too, and I've had a lot of practice. I'll fill in until you get better."

He really wants to do this—and I'm starting to think it's the best option. Even with all the fear I've suffered tonight, I want to trust him. I saw how he is with Molly—and with me.

His name is Brian. He's a hitter for the Cohens, and he wants out as badly as I do. And he has blue eyes and a superhero jaw and an incredible body. He's even good with kids.

Am I dreaming? Have I just lost it? Or is he playing me like the stupid bitch that Toby always said I was?

He wants us to go with him to Mexico. Not for good, just long enough for me to gather my wits and travel somewhere else. But he's made it very clear: until we're out of the States, we're not safe.

"Why do you need us to get across the border? And why California?" I never got to ask questions of Toby. He always told me to keep my damn nose out of his business and left it at that.

"The Cohens have enemies in Southern California. The Milanos. It's even dangerous for me to be there; I've killed some of them." He gulps from his drink and sets the mug aside, using the coaster I've left on the side table.

"That's why you're dyeing your hair and suggesting false IDs? Can you arrange those without the Cohens knowing?" I don't like the idea of him dyeing away the gold in his hair. I try to ignore my preoccupation with his looks, but my mind keeps coming back to them.

I never took pleasure in looking at Toby's body. Wiry, pot-bellied, hairy—like an undernourished ape with the top of his head shaved. He never took the damn glasses off either. Not even when he was fucking me.

I guess not removing them or his clothes or sometimes even his shoes saved him time. He certainly was ... *expedient* ... at sex.

He was also the only man I've ever had sex with. Sex with him was an obligation, a peace offering, as tedious and humiliating as scrubbing a toilet. Each time pacified him for a while, so I put up with it.

I never thought I would run into a man who actually made me want his cock, no matter how crazy or harrowing our situation was. But that's exactly how it is now ... for the first time since my string of high school crushes. Wild, dizzy, badly timed, totally illogical desire.

It's the adrenaline. And I'm drunk on freedom. The bastard's dead—and it's just luck that the man who saved me from him is one glorious piece of beefcake.

"Am I a bad person because I'm glad he's dead?" I ask suddenly, and immediately regret it. My cheeks prickle with embarrassment.

Brian is quiet for a bit. Then he says slowly, "This man abused you. Controlled you. Threatened you. I don't even know what else, but he did it for years, right?"

"Right." My throat's gone tight just thinking about it.

"Then I'm glad the fucker's dead, and I don't give a shit if that makes me a bad person. And neither should you. If you feel better now that he's gone, he must have been the worst damn husband."

The empathy in his voice reminds me of his touch—powerful, but somehow tender, as if he's so aware of his strength that he doesn't want to risk any chance of hurting me. I squeeze my knees together, trying to ignore another surge of desire.

"Thank you," I murmur, and decide to leave the subject be for now. "So ... we go to California, pretend to be a family, cross the border, and then what?"

"There's a resort in Baja where we can stay for a few weeks while you put yourself back together. Then if you want, we can just go our separate ways. You'll have the money you brought with you, and I'll have my freedom." His eyes twinkle.

"But until then, we pretend to be husband and wife to throw off suspicion." I try to ignore just how appealing that sounds. "With Molly as our daughter."

After seeing him in action, I don't doubt his ability to keep up the act of a doting dad. It makes me wonder where he got so good with kids. But pretending to be his wife?

Sharing a bed?

I take a hasty sip from my mug to relieve my suddenly dry mouth. *It's just shock. It's making me think crazy things.*

"That's right. We just pretend to be tourists with our kid, have fun for four-odd weeks, and then once my new retreat is ready and some of the heat is off, we'll decide what happens next." He tilts his head slightly. "What do you think?"

This is all so sudden. Just like Toby's death. And yet ... he's right.

Think fast, Ophelia. This opportunity isn't going to last.

"Can I trust you to keep us out of harm's way?" I could never trust Toby with that. I'm sick of men I can't trust.

"Can I trust you not to break character for the whole trip?" His gaze is steady, challenging.

"Yes. We'll just have to find ways to make this easier for Molly." I chew my lip. I can't believe I'm making plans like this, instead of falling apart in the bathroom for another hour.

There's no choice. I have to be strong for myself and my baby. I just pray I'm making the right choice.

He nods, still firmly gazing at me. "I promise, then. We'll make it as easy as possible for Molly—and for you."

I feel a deep warmth in the pit of my stomach as he says that. I know he's a mob hitter. I know he's probably killed dozens of people for money. But I'm still agreeing to this and making plans. And not just for survival's sake.

Even half numb, even if I fall apart on the road somewhere because of everything going on, I can already feel the crush on mysterious Brian drawing me toward him. I know it's messing with my judgment. But he's also offering me a chance to start over where the Cohens can't possibly reach us.

"Let's get ready, then," I say as calmly as I can.

Please let me be making the right choice.

CHAPTER 5

Brian

WE'VE BEEN on the road for an hour in this rainstorm, and the kid still hasn't asked where her daddy is. That's the thing that sticks out for me the most. Not a word on him—no worry, no curiosity.

She wants to know where we're going: California. She wants to know why we're going: a vacation. She wants to know who I am: Mom's friend, who's helping them.

But there's no "where's my daddy?" or "when are we coming back?" or "why did we go so late at night?" No fear. She dropped off twenty minutes into the drive, face as peaceful as if she was still in her own bed.

What is with this kid? I thought Ophelia said her father doted on her. Is it just normal for him to be gone all the time?

I look in the back seat of the aging, cash-bought sedan we're using as we're stopped at a small-town intersection, and see

Molly curled up, surrounded by stuffed animals. They were each supposed to pack only one suitcase while I was off dropping Daddy's corpse into a hole in the desert, but of course, Molly wanted to bring all her friends.

I wasn't about to argue with her. She wasn't throwing a fit over going somewhere before dawn without her father, and that was worth filling up the back seat with a rainbow of stuffies.

"So I'm guessing Toby didn't have life insurance." I'm hoping she'll be all right financially with him gone.

"No, he never gave much thought to what was going to happen to us, I'm afraid." She sighed and glanced back at her daughter. "I don't even think he had a will. I think he probably would have liked the idea that we couldn't live without him."

"You gonna be okay?" I shouldn't even be asking. It's none of my damn business. I'm helping her get away. She's helping me not leave a trail by coming with. It's enough.

She's an adult. She can take care of herself and her baby. Most of my job is done here. It'll be done once and for all after we cross that border and play family for a few weeks.

But even as I told myself that, I remember the gut-instinct move I made of putting myself between her and her attacker, and know that despite my best efforts, this has already gotten a bit personal.

Wrapping up the job was simple despite the weather. I came out to the site with the body bag, dropped it in the hole, and helped the poor schmuck who was left out in the rain waiting for me to put six feet of dirt over it. We planted a couple of the local rosemary bushes on top and went our separate ways without a word.

I called it in as soon as I dropped off the van and changed back into my jeans and leather jacket. "This is Stone. It's done. No complications."

Jacob stifled a yawn. He was used to calls at insane hours,

and his response was calm and all business. "I'll send the funds. Call back in ten minutes if you don't receive."

Five hundred thousand dollars later, I got back on the road to pick up the ladies. Now we're a fifth of the way to San Diego, with a two-room suite waiting for us at a mid-priced motel. And I'm trying not to worry about their futures in addition with my own.

"It's not going to be a problem. I found ... an awful lot of money in Toby's safes," Ophelia reassures as the light changes and we start forward. "Stacks of hundreds with those paper bands. They're most of what's in my suitcase."

"Oh. You didn't want to bring anything?" I don't ask how much money she has, but it's a big suitcase. You can fit a million dollars in a standard-sized briefcase; what she has sounds like enough for her to restart her life, and that's good enough.

"Toby picked out all my clothes. He threw out or broke everything personal I showed up with. Nothing in my closet was to my own taste except some sleepwear Molly picked out." That soft, flat tone she uses when she talks about what this guy did to her makes me wish I had shot him someplace a lot more painful.

"Besides," she ventures, life trickling back into her voice, "didn't you say we need to change our appearances?"

"We do. So we'll just go shopping when we've had a chance to rest." She'll probably start crying again between here and there, but that's to be expected. "How are you holding up?"

"I ..." She looks out the window at the desert flashing by. We left the storm behind with that last town, and the brightening moonlight was turning the chaparral silver and blue all around us. "I'm still trying to figure out how much I can trust you."

"Well, I guess that's no surprise. It's really the same for me—after all, if you drop the dime on me, I'm done." I keep my voice calm and low, in case the bitty sleeper in back starts to wake up.

"If I drop the dime on you, we're probably both done, and

then Molly will have nobody." She hesitates, then says firmly, "I knew what I was doing. I was desperate to get away from him, not scared of you."

Wow. "I'd say that's pretty ruthless, but like I said before, I don't think you should feel bad. The guy deserved ruthless. I'd have done the same in your shoes." I can't keep a slight edge out of my voice as I talk about it.

"I guess we're just gonna have to learn to trust each other." She laughs nervously, voice rising to a temporary squeak. She has to take a few moments to calm herself after that, and simply follows up with, "But you give a damn, and that helps a lot."

"You seem surprised. Is it my day job?" I put it jokingly, but her laugh reduces to something of a sob and then peters out.

"No, I think I'm just that burned out." She runs her fingers against the window, tracing some of the droplets still clinging to the glass. "A lot of women in my position just stop trusting men altogether. It's simpler."

"And here I am asking you to trust me after I just shot someone in front of you." No wonder she doesn't seem to know what to think or feel right now.

"Yeah, that's a little … tough. But … mostly I'm still getting used to the idea that he's gone. I never … I never expected to walk away from that relationship on my own two feet." She's facing the window fully now; I see her cheeks gleaming in her reflection in the glass and my heart sinks.

"It's okay. We'll get there and you can sleep this off. The last place the Cohens are going to look for me is in Southern California. We'll have a breather for a day or two." It'd be safer if it were less, but I'm dealing with a woman in shock who is trying to figure out her next moves.

"O-okay," she mumbles, then glances at me. "There's something I don't understand, though."

"What's that?" At least she's opening up and asking questions. She's trusted me this far.

"How ... how did a guy like you end up ... in your job?" She practically whispers it.

I let out a laugh. "Oh that? Well ... it's kind of a long, ugly story. But what it boils down to is that I killed a drug dealer in my neighborhood after he kidnapped a local kid. I got caught for it and was going to jail. Then the Cohens showed up and made me an offer."

"And it was that or prison." Her voice strengthens, going thoughtful. "All because you shot a drug dealer."

"I didn't even go there to shoot the bastard," I blurt out. "But that girl was twelve, and he was trying to get her hooked so that she would keep ... coming over. I'm ... not gonna get more detailed than that. But you probably get the idea."

"Yeah, yeah I do." She rubs the tears off her cheeks, lips twisting in disgust. "So you had to come work for them. No choice."

"Having my life ruined because I stepped in where the cops wouldn't, wasn't much of a choice. But you're right—I never wanted this. I've been saving up ever since then, living modestly and waiting for the day I could just get out."

A faint rumble of thunder echoes toward us from the storm we've left behind. It feels like it's chasing us. But the air here is drier; it will peter out before we reach San Diego.

Her voice is still low, but it gains a dull note of jaded suspicion. "If you're just making up some bullshit to make me feel better, thanks, but I'd rather have the truth. Toby lured me in with bullshit, but as soon as he had me, he dropped the act and I ended up hurt. So ... please be blunt."

I suddenly wish I had something stronger to drink than that dollop of coffee liqueur a few hours ago. "I'm not shitting you. I know I screwed up signing on with these guys, but people make bad decisions when they're under that much pressure."

"I know," she cuts in. "I'm sorry if I'm wary. But it's just like you said—I'm under a lot of pressure, and I don't want to make a bad decision." She looks back at her sleeping daughter. "Like I did marrying Toby. The only good thing to come from that is sitting right there behind us."

"I get you. And I know that in a situation like this, I can tell you to trust me, but only my actions are gonna prove that I deserve it. Not anything I say." I'm speeding; I catch myself and ease off the accelerator.

"I don't actually have any secrets like yours." She's looking out the window again when I glance over. "Came to Las Vegas to be a showgirl, ended up a waitress. I wouldn't get on the casting couch, so I couldn't get any performance parts. Toby scooped me up when I was down and desperate."

Man, I'm getting gladder that I shot him the more she talks about him. "That's what predators do. They did it to me. Different circumstance, same method."

She starts to laugh almost silently, tiny coughs and snickers breaking the quiet between us. Of course, when I look over, her eyes are wet again. "That's kind of a messed-up thing to have in common."

"Yeah. But maybe it means we'll judge each other less." I'm hoping so. For all I know, we'll get to California and she'll vanish with her baby before we can carry our plans out. But I keep telling myself *so far, so good* and hoping I'm right.

"I wasn't planning to judge you. Just the ... job, and you're already leaving that." She flinches as lightning flashes somewhere behind us.

Maybe it would have been better if I had stayed in Baja with Jamie and his family. Simply never come back; not taken the risk. Ultimately, though, that half-million was needed to complete my escape plan.

Otherwise, I would have been Jamie's guest for a very long time.

"Yeah. I am. I'm retiring early. The Cohens can go fuck themselves." I say it just as calmly as everything else, and she stifles a laugh in response.

"Just as long as they don't fuck *us* on the way out." She wraps her arms around herself and shivers in the warm car. "At least there's nothing back in Vegas that I have a problem with leaving behind."

"Nothing, huh?"

She looks behind her at her daughter and smiles. "My most precious things are already with me."

She dozes off beside me a while after that, exhausted by the late hour and all the drama. I'm pretty tired as well, so I briefly stop for some caffeine. I burn my mouth on truck-stop coffee for the next half hour until the fog in my head starts to clear.

My burner phone buzzes half an hour later. I ignore it at first. Let them think I'm asleep back in my house in Las Vegas. With all the clothes and goodies that I now have to leave behind.

I didn't expect to have to leave everything behind like that, not so fast. I shipped a lot of the lighter stuff ahead of time, anticipating my escape—but not all. There's maybe fifty thousand in exercise gear, electronics, and sports collectibles in that house that I wish I could have brought with me—but they can be replaced.

My life can't be replaced. Ophelia and her daughter—their lives can't be replaced, either.

But the phone keeps ringing.

Finally, I give up and pull over at the next rest stop to check it. No messages left—just my handler's number. Five times. I get out of the car, lean on my hood, and call Jacob back.

"That took a while," he complains when he picks up.

"Some people sleep. What's going on?" I mute the phone as I catch sight of a semi-truck rumbling toward us. It goes past in a rush of air, and I listen hard for his answer.

"Loose ends. The wife and child are missing from the house. Looks like they took a few things, including suitcases."

I wince and lean back, looking up at the cloud-streaked sky, which is showing signs of lightening in the east. I'm no good at making things up, so I change the story as much as I dare instead.

"When I got there, there was some kind of domestic incident going on. I don't know the specifics, but I do know that the wife and her little girl left in a taxi with a pair of suitcases."

A pause. I tense up, wondering if he's found the hole in the story I just told. But after a while, he simply mutters, "That explains a few things. Did you empty his safes?"

"Man, I didn't even go inside the house. Why, did she clean him out?" It doesn't take much for me to push a laugh into my voice.

"Two big ones. Clean as a whistle inside. Not sure how the target didn't notice. Was he feeling well?"

"Drunk." The word falls from my lips like a stone dropping into a well, hollow and final.

He scoffs. "Well, that would be why he couldn't stop her."

"Yeah, I would say so." I stifle a yawn. "Is there anything else?"

"Just that. How'd you draw him outside in this mess?" His tone has gone calmer, more sociable. Like we're colleagues again suddenly, now that he knows I didn't fuck up the job.

"After she left, it took him all of five minutes to turn on his porn. Then I sabotaged his satellite dish so he would come out to check it." That, they probably already found evidence for.

I've known for a while that the Cohens will send in a cleaner once the killing's done so they can remove any evidence. I didn't realize, however, that the cleaner would be checking up on me as well.

Maybe I should have. Or maybe they suspect something, and they've never actually checked up on me like this before. I have no way of knowing which one, and the thought sends my blood pressure up.

His chuckle suddenly sounds fake to me. "Clever."

"I have my moments. Anyway, I'm drying off after being out in that mess. You have anything else that can't wait?"

How much do they know? How deeply did they check?

Did they follow me out to the job site?

Are they following me now?

No, there's no way. I changed outfits, changed cars, drove from place to place before going back to pick up the girls ... wait. Did they have the house watched? Did they see me pick her up?

My heart starts beating fast and hard, but his voice is as calm as ever when he answers.

"Nothing pressing. The boss will want to see you tomorrow, however. Three p.m. sharp at the Royale. Boardroom, as usual." He's all business again.

"Oh. Okay, I'll be there." That gives me a lead time of less than twelve hours before they start looking for me—if that. *Shit. Shit. Shit.*

He hangs up and I lean against the car for a while longer until I can get my heart rate under control. Ophelia's stressed out enough. I won't tell her what I found out. It's my problem.

We had better get moving, though.

I get back in my car, check on my sleeping passengers, and then start up again, driving as fast as I can without drawing any attention.

CHAPTER 6

I FALL asleep in Nevada and wake up in San Diego with dawn already broken. I blink awake in the gray light and stretch as best I can against the seat belt.

"We're here," Brian says cheerfully as he fights our way through already thick traffic. "How are you doing?"

I do a quick sanity check. The hot stranger beside me killed my husband last night, and we escaped with Toby's money. I'm half complicit; I helped him.

But it's not like Toby didn't give me every reason. Including threatening me because his damn porn channels went out. I can't forgive him for any of it.

Can I forgive myself? Will the Cohens leave me alone?

I look in the back seat. Molly yawns and blinks back at me with droopy eyelids. "Can we get cocoa?" she asks in her fluting voice, completely calm.

"As soon as we're settled." I smile with relief as I look back at Brian. "I'm fine."

"Okay, that's good. I'll get you settled into the room and go out for food." His smile is even more dazzling in sunlight; I knot my fingers together in my lap as another awkward surge of desire goes through me.

This man killed my husband and took me along on his run from the mob. Now I want to fuck him. What kind of woman have I become?

Desperate. A desperate woman protecting herself, protecting her child. The fact that Brian can get me tingling with just a smile is irrelevant.

"Don't forget the cocoa!" Molly insists.

"I won't. I promise. It'll just be a while because I need to get my hair cut." Brian fights a grin for the third time when talking to Molly. It's strange to see. Here's a man who can pull the trigger without hesitation, as long as it's not an innocent person, and here he is ... here he is doting on my child.

Maybe Brian just likes kids. But there are so many differences between his behavior toward Molly and the way Toby was with her that I can't help but think about them as we pull into the hotel parking lot.

Did Toby really treat our daughter well? Or did he just buy her things and ignore her, and compared to what I went through, it looked to me like good treatment? And what is this man doing in comparison?

Is it possible for a killer to be this kind? Or is it an act to get me to trust him? The question keeps coming back to me, and I still don't know how to answer it.

But God, am I glad to have a state line between us and the Cohens now. I'm so eager to leave all that mess behind that I don't even ask what Brian did with Toby's body.

No rain here. Everything's dry and a touch smoggy, the early-morning sky yellowish around the edges. As I get out and stretch, my shoulders pop, and I feel the bruise on my cheekbone as I yawn.

The pain of the bruise leads to the memory of Toby's fist, and the memory of Toby's fist takes me back to that rain-swept lawn, and how my ears rang from the gunshot, and how I forced myself to smile when Toby stared at me with dying eyes.

Am I a terrible person?

Tears suddenly brim in my eyes. I don't care. Maybe I am, but if that's what it takes for Molly and me to be free, that's what I'm going to be. I'll be as wild and terrible as I have to be—including toward Brian if it comes down to it.

But for now, all I can think of is resting in a proper bed with my little girl.

I wipe my eyes before I turn to help her out of the car. She tiredly blinks at me; I see worry on her face and give her a bright smile. "Come on, sweetie, we're going into a hotel room so we can rest better."

"Okay." She grabs her pillow and her purple teddy bear and hops out as I open the door, yawning enormously again. "I still wanna stay up."

"That's fine, but let's shower and change into fresh clothes." I take the pillow and clasp her hand, wary of the busy parking lot.

"Grab all the stuffed animals, too. I'm trading cars later today." Brian is already opening the trunk.

"Sure." I'm amazed by how Brian can stay so focused after being up all night. Military guys get used to insane hours—and hitters must be somewhat the same—but as my knees wobble and my head throbs from my broken sleep, I'm impressed by his control. "Just let me get Molly settled."

Brian easily carries both suitcases as he leads us up the stairs and to our suite. "Sure. What do you like for breakfast? Bagels all right?"

"Sounds, um, good." I look him in the eyes, and every time, it's like staring into the sun. It warms my face and dazzles my eyes, and I have to quickly look away.

I don't think I can trust myself around this man.

He's gotten us a two-room suite. San Diego hotel decór reminds me of Florida: pastels mixed weirdly with earth tones, arched doorways, and ceiling fans in every room. The suite smells faintly of air freshener and cannabis, but no bug spray, mildew, or filth.

"Take the one in the back. I want to be closest to the door in case there's any trouble." He puts it quietly and calmly, but a chill runs down my back.

"I thought you said we would be safe here?" I ask in a hushed voice. Molly is already climbing onto the bed in the back room, eyes almost closed from sleepiness, her demand for cocoa forgotten.

His hand settles on my shoulder, and I turn at his touch, trying to ignore the warmth sinking into my skin. "We're a hell of a lot safer here than we were back in Vegas. But the Cohens aren't stupid, and San Diego has its own problems."

My mouth is dry. I swallow hard and nod. "I'll ... come help get those stuffed animals in now." No point complaining about it; big cities aren't safe. Miami wasn't, Las Vegas wasn't. Why would San Diego be any different?

When we get the last of the stuffies onto the bed surrounding Molly, and Brian has gone to handle his errands, I lock the door behind him. I put the chain on and then push a chair in front of the door and double-check Molly before going to get my shower.

I'm practiced at crying in the shower, where I won't be seen and probably won't be heard over the water. This time, though, as I step into the glassed-in stall, the tears don't flow. Maybe I'm all cried out. I've cried a lot in the last few days.

Or maybe it's because the source of my tears is dead, with his withered little heart splattered all over his back lawn. Toby ... you son of a bitch, you deserved a slower death. But even that thought only makes my eyes sting slightly.

I can't cry over him. I don't have a reason to cry for myself or Molly anymore with him dead. So tears don't fall. But my mind is still racing.

I didn't count all that cash I stuffed in with my clothes and books. I should do that, I realize—and definitely get it done before Brian comes back. But by the time I emerge from the bathroom and open my suitcase, I'm heavy-lidded and yawning almost constantly.

I stare at all those bundles of cash, then sigh and grab the sleeveless eyelet-lace nightgown on top of the clothes pile and pull it on. I'll count it later. Each short stack has ten thousand dollars in it, and there are at least forty of them. I can get by on that for a good while.

I slip under the covers next to my daughter and bury my nose in her hair. She whimpers softly and then rolls over, tucking her head under my chin. "It's okay, sweetie. We're free now."

"Okay," comes the half-awake response, spoken softly into my neck. "Just don't forget my cocoa."

I smile into her hair. I don't know for certain that she's going to be okay; she's been strangely quiet about Toby all night. No "where's Daddy?" or "when do we go home?" ... none of that.

I thought she was pretty attached. She always asked me where Daddy was back home when he was gone. *What's going on in your head, sweetheart?*

But I can barely figure out what's going on in mine. Do I trust Brian? Do I act on my desire for him and get the taste of Toby out of my mouth for good? What do I do now, with all this money and the mob potentially after me—and certainly after Brian?

As I slip off to sleep, I remember again the moment that Toby rushed me, and this man, this killer, this total stranger put his body between me and Toby and pointed a gun at him. The gun was part of his job. But meat-shielding me from my own husband?

That was personal choice. The choice to step in, in a way that I had wished someone would do for me for years. And because of that, I can't get him out of my mind.

Who are you really, Brian? And why do you care so much about a total stranger?

INTERMISSION

Carolyn

"You did this, didn't you?"

Daniels isn't just day-drunk, he's *dawn*-drunk. He's phoning me up at seven in the morning Eastern to scream at me. His voice is slurry and keeps cracking, and I can hear a woman's heels aggressively clacking back and forth on a hardwood floor in the background.

"I'm sorry, sir, what are you talking about? I'm in Las Vegas following up on the Stone case." I know exactly what he's talking about. The hard click-thud of a suitcase being slammed closed in the background confirms it.

His wife's leaving. Right now. Prometheus did exactly what I suspected he would do, and now Mrs. Daniels will be taking her maiden name again—along with half of everything Daniels owns.

And I'm the one who set Prometheus on him like an overprotective dog.

"You know—you already fucking know! Is this your revenge

for me sending you up the coast in winter?" His voice cracks again, like a hysterical teen's.

"Sir, no. I really don't. If you're going to accuse me of something, I'd like to know what it is." Keeping my voice calm and even when I'm worn out, sick of his shit—and vaguely guilty—is taking all my focus.

"You told on me to my wife! You sent that email with all the attachments!" He almost sounds like he's going to cry.

"Sir. I didn't send any emails. I don't even have your personal email address, let alone hers." He doesn't deserve the closure of knowing it was me ... with the help of a vindictive hacker. "The only thing I sent last night was the preliminary update to our file on Brian Stone. To your *work* address."

He goes very quiet. I can hear him gasping in anger as his wife says something in a shrewish tone I don't catch. "I see."

"Do you, sir? Because I'm still trying to sort out why you're phoning me right now." I relax slightly, realizing that he really doesn't have a clue who dropped the dime on him with his wife. I don't know if he's going to level his shouty accusation at every woman in the Bureau who he's sexually harassed ... but it's a good bet.

"I see. Just following up on a ... lead. I'll give more details later. Carry on." And he hangs up the phone so fast, I'm left staring at it in surprise.

I drop the phone onto the pillow beside mine and roll over with a sigh, staring out the window at the gray light seeping through the cloud layer. It's another warmish, rainy February morning; I have a gift box from Prometheus on the table and crucial information likely waiting in my email box, and Daniels' wife is leaving him for his constant attempts to cheat.

Aside from the sleep deprivation and not knowing where the hell my career is going, it's shaping up to be a damn good day.

I look over at the box from Prometheus again, wondering

what he's taken the trouble to send me. Working with Prometheus is like having a benevolent stalker: he makes me nervous but is full of pleasant surprises. I wonder if he simply doesn't know how to approach people normally—or is too wary of having his privacy or freedom taken to do so.

What in the world does a guy like that send as a gift?

I get up, tugging at my nightshirt unconsciously even though I'm alone. I know Prometheus isn't in the room any more than Daniels is, and yet I get a shower and my clothes handled before I even approach that box. I'm getting tired of never knowing where I stand with the men in my life, regardless of relationship.

Not that I know much about the kind of relationship Daniels wanted to have. One of the reasons I've never slept with a man is because so many of them seem to be more or less like him. I don't feel like being exploited or finding out too late that there's a wife in the picture. I took one step down that road once, and I'm not doing it again.

I examine the box. It looks like a bog-standard postal delivery, no over-taping, no staining, no odd smells. I stare at it for a few moments longer, then pull my switchblade from my pocket and cut the box open.

Inside, I find three items: an unlabeled, high-tech-looking black laptop, a matching phone in an almost armored-looking case, and a note. I know the handwriting; he slipped me a similar note back in Massachusetts.

Dear Carolyn,

I know that you must find it strange that I have chosen to watch over you. However, I can only assure you that I mean no harm—quite the opposite, in fact, and I intend to continue proving that until you believe me.

The devices inside are significantly more secure than your Bureau-issued ones and should operate at far higher efficiency.

Using them will provide us with a better connection and will allow me to help you more directly.

Of course, it is up to you whether you use them, but I ask that you not dispose of them, even through sale. They are prototypes and not intended for use by the general public.

I open the laptop tentatively. It's a chunky design, tougher-looking than the practically bendable models that have gotten more and more popular these days. It powers up silently without showing any computer or operating-system logos, and offers a desktop screen so fast that, for a moment, I think it's glitched.

The screen is bare-bones, with a program list that looks to be mostly freeware, and a few folders. I open the email program and connect to the motel's network; this computer's speed already blows my laptop away.

I check the system thoroughly, find nothing amiss aside from its strange speed and total lack of branding, and then check my email on it. A note from Prometheus is waiting for me.

Brian Stone's target was Tobias Whitman, a Cohen accountant who was guilty of significant and obvious embezzlement. He and his family will be reported to the police as having disappeared within the next few days.

Tobias is dead. His wife and daughter are with Stone, currently on the way to San Diego.

He's headed for Baja California again. But why bring the woman and girl? Hostages? I read on, my confused frown deepening as I go.

Unfortunately, my sources within the Cohen organization have indicated to me that Brian is already under suspicion due to the coercive nature of his recruitment, his refusal to kill innocents, and his recent lengthy vacation. Because of this, I am nearly certain that he is being followed by a Cohen-employed hitter who is well aware of his vacation haunts. The hitter will be targeting the woman and girl as well, as they are witnesses.

Baja California is well outside your jurisdiction, of course. However, two innocent American citizens are in harm's way—and the assassin being sent after him will wish to return to the States afterward, regardless of whether he or she is successful.

The address included below is the resort which Stone will be staying at under an assumed name. If I determine the identity of the assassin, I will send you that information as quickly as possible. Their exact location in San Diego cannot be determined, but you may be able to catch them at the border.

Good luck. If the assassin after Stone is who I think he is, you will need it.

San Diego. At least it's a shorter flight to someplace warm. I can only hope that the guy filling in for Daniels will approve the change of venue before Stone slips away altogether.

CHAPTER 7

Brian

For the first time in a long time, I wish that I could open up to Jamie and let him know what exactly I'm escaping from in the States. There's no chance of that happening ... but I really could use a second opinion on my current course of action. Especially the fact that I'm not fleeing the Cohens alone.

I've always lived by my instincts, and they said to take Ophelia and Molly so that the Cohens don't find out what they know and kill them to prevent anything getting back to the cops. That is standard procedure with them, and I damn well know it. It seemed like a good idea to take them with me, and certainly the right thing to do, but now ...

Now, things are getting complicated. I've got a traumatized abuse survivor and her enigmatic, weirdly resilient kid to look after, and to make it worse, I can't stop thinking about Ophelia.

The thing I hate most about living life on the criminal side is seeing innocent people get hurt. No matter how "victimless" the crime, whether drugs or gambling or legal brothels, someone is always getting hurt behind the scenes. I have to see that way too much and pretend it doesn't bother me.

Stepping in when my target threatened Ophelia was instinct. Spending five hours on the road getting a boner off and on just from the smell of her perfume is ... a much less convenient or logical instinct. Fun as it was to flirt with her to break the tension, my attraction to her is affecting my judgment.

"All right, Mr. Smith, you're done," the barber says cheerfully. I open my eyes to take in the brightly colored salon, and then turn to the mirror to look at myself with my new hair, eyebrows rising.

It's the exact same shade of chestnut as Molly's hair. I've gotten extensions to change the length and make it stick up less. I had to talk the reedy, barely-an-adult barber out of shaving my sides—twice. I'm sick of these trendy-ass hipster haircuts that make guys look like their skulls are two feet long.

"That'll do, thanks." I slap a twenty on the counter as a tip on my way out, absently glancing around at the other patrons on the way. The sidewalk is clogged with people in shorts and sundresses, sporting tans in midwinter. There's not so much as a light jacket in sight. We're back in the land of the sun—not as far southwest as I'd like to be right now, but close.

I haven't gotten any further messages from the Cohens since early this morning. I'm hoping nobody's gotten curious and gone by my house. All I need is a day or two's lead to get across the border. I seriously doubt the Cohens will send anyone into Mexico after me.

After all, the cartels are even less friendly to them than rival mob families.

When I get back to the hotel, I have new clothes, dyed hair, a new car to look at for a cash purchase that evening, and a local contact working on fake paperwork for the three of us. I paid through the nose for that last one, but it was worth it. The last thing we need is to get stopped at the border.

When I come in with my bags, the door to the other bedroom is closed. There's a rustle and a sigh and then the thump of Ophelia's feet on the floor as she gets out of bed. I hear a grating sound, like furniture being moved on the thin carpet. The door opens and Ophelia peeks out—and then blinks up at me in surprise.

I give her a smile. "What do you think? I wouldn't let them give me a fade."

"Those look weird with straight hair anyway. It looks good. Kind of ironic, though. We've traded hair colors." She touches her blonde locks absently.

"You're not a natural blonde?" I'm not disappointed, just surprised.

"I'm a Vegas blonde, honey. Show runners don't hire brunettes. And Toby got mad if I so much as let my roots show." There's a flash of sad frustration in her eyes. "I've thought about dyeing it back now."

"Maybe a good idea. They'll be looking for two blonds, after all, if anyone comes after us." And the more we can throw off their scent, the better.

She's wearing a knee-length sleeveless nightgown. It clings to her thighs as she moves toward me. I have to tear my gaze away, so it doesn't get stuck exploring her curves.

"I need to ask you something important," she says over my suddenly pounding heart.

"Shoot." I sit down on the edge of the bed and start going through the shirts, underwear, and jeans I bought, stripping their tags off and folding them for my suitcase. I've had enough of wearing mook suits when I'm not wearing disguises.

"How ... long will Molly and I have to be in hiding?" The

worry in her voice edges on real fear. "Before they won't come after us?"

"Not long, likely. A month, maybe two, before they figure you were running from your husband and not them and decide you're not a liability. After that ... do you have anything to go back to Vegas for? Because it's not the best idea for you." I pull socks out of a package and start pairing them.

"Just one friend. But she already thinks I left town to go to a domestic violence shelter." She smiles, but her fingers are twined together in her lap like she's praying.

I nod ... but tense up inside. "Did you tell her where you're going?" I ask quickly.

"I said 'leaving town with Molly and a friend.' Nothing more than that." Her brows draw together, and she pales a little. "Was that bad?"

"Probably not." But my worry just keeps increasing as I think about it. It technically corroborates what I told the Cohens ... but what if they actually check the local shelters?

Troublesome. Risky. The timing has to be suspicious to them.

She pulls over one of the chairs to sit in while we talk.

"You doing okay?" I keep asking that. But she doesn't seem okay—just like she's good at enduring things.

"Better than I was." She sits, crossing her legs; I try to ignore how the lace rides up one sleek thigh. "I actually blocked the door while you were gone, but then realized I wouldn't be awake to open it for you. I did the bedroom door instead."

"You usually block the door when you're going to sleep?" I ask quietly, holding the last pair of socks without sparing the attention to roll them together.

"When I want to feel safe and I'm not forced to sleep beside the source of the problem, yeah. I do. And I don't know this city." She looks away nervously.

"You don't know me either, really. It's okay. How's the tyke?" I'm staring at her smooth thigh again. I go back to rolling socks to try and distract myself.

"She's slept an awful lot. Peacefully. That's ... unusual for her. It makes me wonder." She doesn't seem to notice my roving eyes. Maybe she's too tired.

"Is she usually a light sleeper?" *She noticed something's off, too. Good.*

"If I'm not in with her, she's up at least three times a night." Ophelia glances back at the closed bedroom door. "It started about a year ago."

And then I kill her dad and take her and her mom away, and suddenly she's sleeping like she's making up for lost time. Does she feel safer away from there?

"Mind if I ask you something really personal?" I pull an energy drink out of one of the shopping bags and offer it to her before grabbing one for myself.

"Um, okay." She peeks at me from behind her lashes, and I almost drop my drink. She has no idea how fucking sexy she is even when she's stressed out and half awake.

That bastard Toby had gold in his hands and treated her like garbage. I cough into my fist. "I know that abusive guys don't start out abusive. They kinda work their way up to it, usually over years. How recently did he start hitting you regularly?"

Her jaw drops and all color leaves her face, and I immediately regret asking. "About a year," she says in a voice so tiny that even sitting across from her, I can barely hear it.

She makes the connection at the same time I do, and her eyes brim over with tears. "I tried so hard to shield her from what was going on ..."

Oh shit. Dammit, Brian, what did you go and do? I reach out and take the can out of her shaky hand before she drops it and clasp it in both of mine. "Hey, hey, I'm sorry. I shouldn't have brought it up."

Unfortunately, the floodgates are already open. She buries her face in her hands and starts to sob. "I'm a bad mom! She could only sleep when we got away from him!"

"Kids are observant. It's really not your fault—" I try, but she's bent with her face to her knees now, shaking and weeping uncontrollably.

Nice job breaking her, dumbass. "Holy shit. I'm sorry. C'mere. It'll be okay." I scoop her up and pull her into my lap on the bed. She buries her wet face in my neck and clings to me in response, sniffling.

She smells so good. Citrusy and sweet, some expensive body wash that's probably sold in glass bottles with metal pumps. Under it, the warm musk of a woman, making me crave her even more.

I cradle her and murmur reassurances, and pray I'm doing the right thing. She does seem to be calming down. I just hope she doesn't notice what having her close to me is doing to my body. The crotch of my jeans feels three sizes too tight.

"It's okay," I tell her. "You're free, you're away from him, and soon you'll be free of the Cohens as well. You and your daughter are safe. I won't let anything happen to you."

I don't actually know if I can keep that promise. I couldn't keep it for my mother. But then again ... I was about Molly's age at the time.

The memory gnaws at me briefly. I haven't visited Mom's grave in Montana for months. I'd do it more often, but the old man still lives in that tiny town, getting drunk and whining that his son doesn't love him.

I don't. But nobody in that town, nobody who knew my mother and knows what happened, blames me for that. Only him—because nothing is ever his fault. Not even murder.

I cuddle Ophelia until her tears dry up, ignoring the surges of lust that hit when she shifts on my lap. It takes a while, but by the end of it, her arms are around me and she's not shaking anymore. I stroke her hair, and when she finally raises her face to me, she's blushing and looks ashamed.

"I'm sorry," she mumbles, and I lay a finger over her soft little lips.

"Shhh. It's okay. You're okay. There's no shame in crying over something this fucked up." I want to caress her lips with my finger, but draw it away instead, tapping her gently on the chin.

She smiles shyly up at me, not moving away. But then her gaze dips and she swallows. "How do you ... know so much? About what Toby did. About ... all of that."

"My mom," I say simply. Her eyes widen. I nod, not elaborating. "You have to understand—kids are gonna notice when there's a problem. Even small kids. They may not know what's wrong, but they'll feel it.

"I didn't know what my dad was doing exactly when I was knee-height, but I knew my Mom was scared of him and was sad all the time. And I knew it was his fault. But I didn't know how to ask about it or what to do."

I've never told anybody about this my whole damn life. It makes my stomach clench like a fist, but she's relaxing. It seems to be helping to know things from the kid's point of view—even if the kid's grown up to be a big guy who can kill and wants to protect her.

Then she hugs me so tight that I freeze for a moment, not sure how to respond. "Thank you," she whispers against my neck—and I can feel it down to my toes.

"It's okay, honey, seriously. He's gone. I've only been gladder to have killed a man once—but it's more important that I got you and Molly away from him before ..." My throat tightens and I go quiet.

She slowly raises her head, her eyes bright and soft as they fix on mine. I can tell she understands. Maybe not fully, but enough to know: there was no grown-up around to help my mother get away.

"So that's why…" she whispers, gazing up at me like she's completely dazzled.

"Yeah." With the crisis and crying over, I'm getting more and more aware of her body against mine, her fast heartbeat against my chest, her scent filling my nostrils. My hand has stilled in her hair, cupping the back of her skull.

When she leans forward and brushes her lips shyly against mine, desire detonates inside me, and everything else sweeps out of my mind.

CHAPTER 8

O*phelia*

SOME DECISIONS CAN'T BE TAKEN BACK. You can't very well claim that you didn't mean to kiss someone.

But I've never had a man respond to being kissed for the first time the way that Brian does. He shudders like he hasn't touched a woman in months; his grip tightens on me, and he lets out a low sound like a purr as his lips start caressing mine.

Shame, guilt, fear—they all wash away as we kiss, bodies pressed together, my thighs straddling him now. I don't even remember when that happened or when his hands started caressing me through my nightgown.

I whimper against his mouth as he darts his tongue against mine. My breath stutters to a stop for a moment as his hand slides up my thigh. Deep in my head, a little voice is saying, *"Toby is barely dead and this man killed him,"* and for a moment, it makes me pause.

But then I lean into the kiss again fiercely, defiantly, as if I'm hitting out against Toby's memory. *Good. I want to make him disappear—especially the memory of him touching me. I'll fill my head up with memories of Brian instead.*

His hand slides up to the top of my thigh and around under me, squeezing my inner thigh in a way that makes me squirm and tingle. I'm not wearing panties; self-consciousness pricks at me for a moment as his fingers slip on my already wet skin. I don't care if I seem slutty right now—just as long as he doesn't stop.

He scoops me into his arms again and starts turning, ready to lay me out on that bed. I swoon, not just willing but almost desperate to feel his naked skin against mine. But he's barely set me down when there's a soft cry from the other room.

We both freeze. Brian's grip on me loosens, and he breaks the kiss, looking at the door.

"Mommy?" Molly's call is high and nervous. Not a surprise: strange bedroom, strange circumstances.

Suddenly embarrassed, I sit up as Brian backs off and stands. I can see disappointment in his eyes, but he does so gracefully, going to sit in the chair I abandoned. "Out here, sweetie. Everything's fine."

I get up, tugging my nightgown to my thighs again, and give Brian an apologetic cheek-kiss on the way to comfort my baby. I open the door and see her sitting up in bed, clutching as many stuffies to her as her arms can hold, blinking at me. "I woke up and you were gone," she worriedly chirps.

"I was just in the next room, sweetie." I climb into bed with her and put an arm around her. She leans on me, relaxing.

"Okay. Just don't leave me behind. I don't want to be alone." I can see tears on her cheeks, and I hug her more tightly.

"That will never happen, Molly. I promise." I kiss her temple and she smiles.

As for Brian ... I'll come back to our little "discussion" next time she's asleep.

It takes the rest of the day to get everything ready for our trip to Mexico. Brian takes me around, buying me clothes and shoes, getting my hair straightened and dyed back to its original color. It feels like I'm coming back to myself: my old hair, my old outfit of jeans and a flowing blouse, underwear that doesn't cram itself half up my ass by design.

Molly gets new clothes, too, though she had brought along more of hers. I don't want her to feel left out—though I do draw the line on letting her get pink hair at the salon. Brian finds her a bright orange dog to go with her other stuffies, and she runs around with it and her love-worn purple bear for the rest of the day.

One worry nags at me as we dash around. I'm still carrying the tingle that Brian's almost desperate kisses left inside me. Will he like me less now that I'm no longer trying for Vegas-showgirl glamour?

He still looks at me with that gleam in his eyes, though, and he still stays close to me as often as he can, like he's drawn to me magnetically. That soothes my doubts, leaving me to enjoy the freedom of running around in flats and comfortable clothes for the first time since I got married.

I don't know how I ever managed to chase Molly in those damned stripper heels Toby insisted on all the time. My feet are getting sore in places I'm not used to, but it's worth it.

Molly is smiling, laughing, refreshed from getting adequate sleep for once. She talks to her new orange doggie and runs around in the park where we stop for a late picnic lunch. And never—not once—does she bring up her absent father.

How much do you know, baby girl? How much did you pick up from body language, mysterious bruises, and far-off arguments? I'll have to talk to her about this ... but until we're more recovered, it doesn't seem like a good idea.

I'm glad that Brian understands—really understands—in a raw way that I could never have imagined. I'm almost certain that his mother is dead by his father's hand, and he didn't want to bring up specifics. Of course he didn't.

Around sundown, he takes us to a small lot on the outskirts of town to pick up the new car. He has us wait in the old one while he goes to deal with the rangy redhead in the grimy coveralls who leans casually against the big, blocky vehicle. I hold Molly's hand the whole time and try to ignore the strangers walking past on the filthy sidewalk nearby.

The two talk like old friends for a few minutes, the tall stranger grinning and bobbing his head. Brian points at the car we're sitting in; the man nods and holds up three fingers. Just for a moment, as I watch this shady transaction in this shady place, I'm reminded again that my semi-hero and lust-object may be trying to retire ... but he's still a criminal.

I'm a terrible judge of character. I know that from my letting Toby draw me in the way he did. What if I'm wrong about Brian, too? What if he's not selling the car ... but us?

No, that's ridiculous. I'm being paranoid. I already know he's leagues better than Toby ever dreamed of being.

"Are you okay, Mommy?" Molly asks at my elbow. "Does your face hurt?"

My hand flies up to the almost faded bruise. I didn't even know that she noticed it under my makeup. Saddened, I shake my head. "No, it's almost healed now. I'll be okay, sweetheart."

She nods with a tiny, thoughtful frown, and then looks over at Brian as he hands a thick envelope to the man, who peers inside and then bobs his head again. "Did Brian save us from Daddy?"

My stomach drops. I'm not ready for this. But here she is

asking it, and I need to provide an answer that won't freak her out but isn't a lie, either.

"Yes," I murmur, even as Brian comes walking back to us. "Yes, he did. We're going somewhere where Daddy can't find us."

She doesn't cry or throw a fit; she just looks up at me solemnly. "I'm glad. He was mean and he hurt you."

I close my eyes on tears and nod silently, too overcome to speak.

CHAPTER 9

Brian

It's a warm night even for San Diego as we join the long line for the border checkpoint. The giant old Ford sedan that Jamie's buddy Willy sold me is scarred and ugly, but it runs solid and is comfortable inside. Molly chatters away in the back as we wait for our turn.

I'm not that worried that the security officials will see through our new identification papers. They're good quality, and we give every appearance of being a typical American family escaping cold weather by going on vacation. Besides ... it's getting back into the US that's usually the problem, and I don't plan to do that for years, if at all.

"Where will you go after the resort in Baja?" Ophelia asks me as she hands Molly an open bottle of orange juice.

"I've got a place. I've been working on it for years—my hideaway from everything. It's off the coast in international waters.

It's not ready yet or we could just go there." I debated telling her about the island before now, but after that kiss ... after the ugly secrets we've shared ... I don't want to let her go.

I know I'm not thinking straight. I don't really care. But I'm working my way up to inviting her and her little girl to the island hideaway where I once believed I would live alone. I don't know if it's for keeps. If we're lucky, and we get along for the month in Baja, maybe it can be.

"You have a private island?" Her eyebrows climb as I fight a grin. I already know it doesn't take much beyond real kindness to impress Ophelia after all she's been through, but it's gratifying to see her quietly blown away by something I've accomplished.

"Well, it's not very big or luxurious, but it has all the essentials, and in a month, it'll have a house with wind, solar, and water collectors." Also top-notch security, a year's worth of food and supplies, radio contact with the mainland, and a dock for my boat. "If things work out, I'll give you a tour."

"I'd like that." Ophelia still isn't blinking enough, and I chuckle as I refocus on driving to the next space in line.

"Have you thought about what you want to do after this?" Maybe it's too soon to ask that. But I'm hopeful that I can improve her opinion of me enough that she'll want to stay.

"I just ... don't know. I always thought that if I moved away somewhere, it would be in the States. And I guess it still can be, but ... I don't know where yet, or how." She takes a swallow from her own bottle. "Guess I'll have a month to sort it out."

"No family?" She doesn't act like she's leaving anyone behind; as far as I know, she's only called the one neighbor. I hope she was truthful about not telling her friend where she was going or with whom. But then again, she didn't have much information to leak at the time.

"Nobody worth going back for," she mumbles after a

moment, her eyes avoiding mine in that way they do when the subject turns ugly.

"I get it." I wonder if her family was as dramatic as mine, but I know better than to ask. She relaxes when I don't bug her for details. "The resort's maybe two hours down the coast."

I don't tell her that I'm still a touch nervous about the crossing. I don't tell her that I get a bit tenser with every progressive car-length we make, inching closer and closer to the checkpoint. My stomach's jumping; I've never been comfortable making the crossing, and I made it recently enough that I'm worried someone will recognize me despite the change in my looks.

That's ridiculous, though. What are the chances that the same two guys are on this shift, too? *Calm down.* We're almost through. And then I won't have to worry about the Cohens sending someone after me anymore.

At least ... that's a *mostly* safe assumption. I made the reservations under the fake name that's on my new ID, one I have never used before. Not very many people know that I vacation in Baja —and I doubt anyone from the Cohens knows that or will know who to ask about it.

This is the risky part. Right here. If I can get into Mexico, we'll be fine. Just play it cool.

"It's hot here. The rain's gone." Molly presses her cheek against her window and peers out. The car beside us has an aging golden retriever in the backseat who bounces and wags and paws at the window when he sees her. "Ooh, big doggie! I like it here."

"You'll like it better once we get to the resort," Ophelia promises her cheerfully, then stifles a yawn. "Though I think we'll mostly need to sleep when we get there. Or I will."

"I'm not sleepy," Molly insists, then yawns as well. "Oh oops."

I can't help but smile as I pull forward again. Two more cars to go and then we'll be in Mexico, and I can relax a little. And then ...

I wonder if Ophelia will mind much if I interrupt her sleep for a while. My smile widens slightly.

I'm almost relaxed enough to get through this without a hitch when the hairs on the back of my neck stand up. I suddenly feel like I'm being watched, and I don't know why. I look around at both people and cameras, but neither eyes nor lenses are angled my way. So why this feeling?

"What is it?" Ophelia is suddenly watching me closely.

I had to get rid of the gun I did the hit with. I have a cache on the other side of the border I can arm myself from, but until I get there, I've got nothing outside of a boot knife. I keep looking around, eyes narrow. "I don't know. Maybe just going through the checkpoint is bothering me."

"I'm a little nervous, too," Ophelia murmurs, touching my arm lightly.

I nod and pat her hand, giving a tight smile. But I can't relax, and I can't pretend to be relaxed that convincingly anymore, either. I've always been a bad liar, and my acting skills have their limits.

Molly is playing peekaboo with the very excited dog, while the retirees in the front seat chuckle and beam. All around us, sleepy tourists wait for their turn at the window. Nothing out of the ordinary.

I've made the crossing at San Ysidro a dozen times. You show your passport, fill out a tourist permit, then drive through. They want to know where you're going, which means I have to give them the resort name.

I debate lying about it or being general and just saying we're going to Baja. But I'm already at my limit. Appearing legit is important, and there's nothing suspicious about going to a resort. Besides, it's not like the Mexican authorities are going to come looking for me.

So when it's our turn, I bite the bullet, smile, and fill out the damn form while Ophelia fills hers out beside me. I double-check that the names from our IDs are on the forms instead of our real ones, then pass them over to the thin young man with an epic mustache, who looks them over and then stamps us and sends us through.

And that's it. A minute later, we're on the road to Tijuana, with no problems at all. Molly waves bye-bye to the doggie, and off we go.

But the feeling of being watched follows me into Mexico and doesn't fade for several minutes.

CHAPTER 10

Ophelia

The resort at Ensenada is light years away from Vegas. No neon, no crowds, and even though it's not much warmer here than back home, the humid breeze feels like a caress. The room was prepaid, and we called ahead, so they took our late arrival without a fuss. Now I stand on a broad stucco balcony staring out at the Pacific and let relief wash over me.

We got away.

Everything's very quiet right now. Molly is asleep again, snoozing in her own room on the far side of the suite. I just woke up a few minutes ago; Brian left a note saying he's gone out to find us some burritos. I don't know where he plans to get them at close to midnight, but he knows the area a lot better than I do.

I trust him to handle it. Maybe I'm trusting him too much. Depending on him too much. But so far, I've needed to—and so far, he's come through every time.

Then there's the matter of that kiss ... and where it very nearly headed. When he comes back, Molly will be asleep, and we'll be alone and safe for the first time in days. The idea makes my stomach flutter.

I've never wanted anyone like this before in my life. With Toby, it was all obligation and peace offerings. This is a bone-deep craving, as primal and essential as the need for water or air.

Which means it's screwing with my judgment, just like desperation did with Toby. That's dangerous. I need to be smart. For Molly's sake, if not my own.

But I just can't seem to stop the giddy anticipation from simmering away inside of me. My nipples are tight; my pussy aches with the need to be filled. It's getting hard to think of anything else, let alone fight the feelings off.

I don't know how long Brian has actually been gone, but just as I'm starting to worry, keys rattle in the lock on the front door. He walks in looking tired, carrying not only a paper bag stuffed full and spotted with grease, but also what looks like a foot locker tucked under his arm. He gives me a smile as he locks the door behind him and then goes over to the small table, setting both down.

"What's that?" I ask, eyes locked on the box. It's old-looking and battered, its desert camouflage paint job chipped and scratched.

"Insurance," he replies, unpacking the bag onto the table. The first thing out is a tinfoil-wrapped burrito so enormous that it lands on the tabletop with an audible thud. "Just in case something happens."

I tear my eyes away from the whale-sized meals he's unpacking and reach for the locker. He puts a hand over mine. "You know how to use a gun?" he asks, voice suddenly serious.

"Oh." I drop my hand. "No, I barely know where the safety is."

"Do you want to learn?" His eyes catch mine, and I pause, actually thinking about it.

"Maybe. Meanwhile, could you please put that up where Molly can't reach it?" Of course he isn't going to feel safe without a gun around. Meanwhile, I'm wondering if it makes me feel safer or *less* safe.

But I definitely feel safer with him around, even if we had to run to another country to avoid his ex-bosses.

"Of course." He puts the foot locker up on a shelf above the television, and we move any opportunity-presenting furniture out of reach. Molly's small, but agile and determined. Then he flops into a chair at the table. It creaks under his weight as he grabs a burrito and unwraps the end.

The savory smell hits my nostrils, and my mouth starts watering. I sit across from him as he takes an enormous bite. "Can't believe you found a place open this late."

"Not the hardest. We're not exactly off in the countryside here." He winks and slides one of the burritos my direction. "Here, put this in your mouth. If you think you can handle it."

I roll my eyes at him and grab the burrito. "You just *had* to make the joke, huh?" I unwrap the end of mine and take a bite: hot, meaty, and just spicy enough to sting a little. Perfect.

"Yeah, well, I'm basically twelve when it comes to dick jokes. Sorry." He's not, and I just snort and shake my head.

"I'll survive. That would have flown over Molly's head anyway." I try not to eat too fast, but just like my hunger for him, my stomach feels like an empty cavern inside of me. I go quiet for a bit as I get a few more bites in me.

"She sleeping?" There's a faint gleam in his eye as he takes another enormous bite of his own.

"Yeah, deep and sweet. She never sleeps like this." I'm

grateful and ashamed at once. How could I have missed just how much what Toby was doing affected her? Maybe dealing with him left me under too much stress to think completely straight.

"Oh good," he says without elaborating, a naughty smile curving his lips before he takes another chomp of his food.

Oh. I swallow, feeling my cheeks prickle even as I squeeze my thighs together hard under the table. I don't know exactly what he has planned for me, but I know it will start with taking up where we left off.

I try to get myself to make a joke, keep the banter flowing, but the words catch in my throat. He chuckles at my attack of shyness and reaches over to brush a grain of rice off my cheek.

"You are really something else, honey. Don't worry ... I won't bite. Hard, anyway." He winks, and I look down, cheeks hot.

How can he make me feel like a teenage girl again with just a smile and a little flirting? Maybe I've just been starved for so long that it seems like a foreign language. It's been so long since someone proposed sex with more than a "get upstairs and get your clothes off."

Sex itself has always been a letdown but being flirted with by someone this attractive for the first time in forever sends a nice warm glow through me. I smile at him shyly and the gleam in his eye intensifies.

I want him. Even if it's frustrating, even if it hurts a bit, I want him inside me. "Okay," I murmur.

"Sorry, what was that?" His voice has gone gentle, but still teases me. "You're not too shy to play, are you, Ophelia?"

The bite of burrito goes dry in my mouth, and I swallow it with difficulty. "No, it's just ... been a long time." Not since sex, but since I wanted it. But that's depressing, so I don't go into explaining it.

"Well," he purrs, setting his burrito on the table. "Let's fix that."

I manage a tiny nod, but I'm half frozen from nerves.

He stares at me for a moment, then pushes out of his chair and comes around, moving up behind me. His hand settles on my shoulder. "C'mere."

I rise and turn a shy look on him; his smile quirks and then he tugs me into his arms. I relax a little against him, running my hands up his chest. His heart is beating even faster than mine. It shocks me. I'm not used to being wanted by anyone worth wanting.

But memories of gropey, demanding teen fuckboys, of smirking casting directors and scowling show runners, of Toby with his blunt demands, all fall out of my head as Brian kisses me. Suddenly being kissed is this wild, new thing, intoxicating me and leaving me trembling.

I shiver with delight as he scoops me into his arms and carries me to the bed, settling me onto it and kissing me again as he bends over me. His tongue teases around inside my mouth as he impatiently unbuttons his shirt and strips out of it. My fingertips map the muscles of his back and sides, tracing every slab and crease, trailing down to the mounds of his ass as a tremor of delight goes through him.

We hastily undress, kicking off shoes, tossing my blouse into the corner, fumbling out of our jeans as we devour each other's mouths. The whole time, we're trying to stay as quiet as possible, always aware of Molly snoozing in her bed just one door away.

I roll over and raise my ass to get out of my jeans; he lets out an appreciative growl and pulls them off me, then bends over me and starts rubbing and kneading my ass through my panties.

"Goddamn. You're beautiful," he mutters worshipfully as his

fingertips dig firmly into my flesh, sending shock waves of pleasure through me.

He strokes and kisses my back, running his tongue up my spine, grazing me with his teeth and leaving hickeys on the backs of my thighs while I clutch the coverlet and groan into a pillow. He unhooks my bra, tugs my panties down, and starts running his mouth over the freshly bared skin as he tosses the last of my clothes away.

I'm aching. My breasts tingle and my pussy throbs with the need for him.

"Roll over when you're ready," he pants, voice gone hoarse with desire. I look over my shoulder and see him stripping off a pair of boxer briefs, his thick cock bouncing free as he yanks them down.

He goes into the pocket of his jeans for a condom, then rips the packet open and rolls the length of black latex onto himself. He's so excited that I can see his hands shaking and the way his erection jumps a little with his heartbeat.

I work up my nerve and roll over, sitting up against the mound of pillows piled against the headboard. He bends over me and kisses me again, huge hands covering my breasts and stroking them. He rolls my nipples between his fingers as I thrash and throw my head back against the pillows; my eyes roll closed, and I feel the bed bounce as he climbs onto it.

When he takes his hand away from my breast, and his mouth closes hot and wet over it, I bite my lip to keep from crying out. He suckles me in long pulls while his hands explore me. Struggling to keep quiet, I clutch his head, pressing against him, eager for more sensation.

He obliges, pulling harder, tongue flicking against me. I shake, whimpering pleadingly as my back arches. He wraps an arm around me to pull me close, and I feel his teeth tease against my skin, adding an edge to my pleasure.

"More," I whisper.

He switches breasts, the head of his cock rubbing against my thigh as he kneels between my legs. I'm losing track of time, losing all shyness, all hesitation. The insides of my thighs go slick with my juices. He dips two fingers into it and then slides them up between the lips of my pussy.

He strokes his fingers up and down as he switches breasts, sending a jolt of even more intense sensation through me every time his fingertips slide over my clit. Up and down, up and down, his strokes growing faster, until finally he works his way up to my clit again and stays there, circling slowly.

Electric sparks of pleasure roll through me, from nipple to clit and outward through my whole body, making my pussy flutter and clench with the need to be filled. I've never felt this good in my life—or this unapologetically horny.

"I want you inside of me," I gasp hoarsely.

He raises his head, his eyes so wild, they look blind. Then he takes hold of me, lifting me onto his powerful thighs. He takes his cock and works it into me slowly; his girth stretches me in unfamiliar ways, and I gasp and have to cover my mouth with a hand to muffle my long, cooing cries.

Finally, buried inside of me, he kisses me, then starts working his fingers against my clit again. I start to shake harder; there's a pressure mounting up in me. My pussy tightens around him; my clit tingles and aches as he swirls his finger. I open my mouth for his tongue and then groan against his lips as my hips start bucking reflexively with each stroke of his fingertips.

I cling to him with all my strength. His mouth captures mine just as a startled cry escapes me, and his hand starts moving faster. The intensity almost scares me. Something in me wants to retreat from it, as if it might overwhelm me entirely.

But I don't back down. And he doesn't stop. And a moment later, the pleasure mounts until I'm shimmying against him wildly, pushing harsh grunts of joy from his throat that I can barely hear over my heart.

Oh ... what is this ...

I go rigid, shaking, as something detonates inside of me and sends tidal waves of ecstasy crashing outward from my clit. It rolls through my body, making me shake and sob into his mouth as I drown in pleasure.

When the last contraction ebbs away, he stops stroking me and raises his lips from mine. "You okay?" he asks, checking in, voice raspy with need.

"Oh ..." I whisper. "Oh yes ... please don't stop."

He grins ferally. "Good, because no way am I done with you yet."

CHAPTER 11

Brian

I haven't held on this long with a woman in years. She's trembling against me, limp arms thrown around me, legs still twined with mine as I move as slowly as I can force myself. Her hot, slick pussy embraces me again and again, and I ache to speed up and climax, but I don't want this to end.

She moans in my ear, her muscles starting to tighten around me again as I stroke the hood of her clit with my thumb. "Don't stop ..." she whimpers as I circle my thumb over and over. Her trembling becomes rhythmic jerks of her hips as she starts to pant; I brace myself as her eyes close and her head falls back.

"Aah! Ah—" I muffle her with my mouth before she can scream; she shimmies against me hard, her contractions almost milking the climax out of me. I drive the nails of my free hand into my thigh to distract myself. It barely works. Her muffled squeal is music to my ears.

Finally, she collapses, sliding down the pillows a little as I start moving again. She's so relaxed, so exhausted, that she can barely keep her eyes open. Her hands slide over my sweat-slick skin, tracing the bunched muscles in my back as I grind against her.

Panting through my teeth, all my attention focusing on the rising sensations in my groin, I start moving faster. The room blurs in my vision until I squeeze my eyes closed; Ophelia squirms under me, raising her hips against mine with the last of her strength as I bear down on her.

"Oh, Brian," she sobs, clinging to me—and somehow, it's her moan of bliss as much as her sweet embrace that puts me over.

I throw my head back, hissing my breath in and out through clenched teeth as the whole world whites out, and I empty myself in long spurts. "*Yes*," I groan before I can bite it back—and then muffle my moans in the side of her neck. For a split second, it's so intense that it's almost painful ... and then ...

I drift back to proper consciousness blissfully; I'm lying in her arms, head on her shoulder, while her stroking fingers send tingles through the skin of my back. "Unh," I groan, lifting my full weight off her—barely remembering to grab the condom as I pull out, so it won't slip off.

She lets out a small gasp of disappointment as I withdraw. I kiss her gently and then get up and lumber over to the bathroom to dispose of the rubber, moving on wobbly legs. I'm high as a kite from the strongest orgasm I can remember; every step sends fresh tingles through me. When I turn on the bathroom light, my hair is mussed, my eyes slightly glazed, and my smile lazy.

I get rid of the used rubber, wrapping it in toilet paper and shoving it deep into the trash so Molly won't see it. I'm not ready to explain condoms, semen, or sex to a six-year-old. At least we didn't wake her up.

When I come back, some of my bliss vanishes as I see Ophelia balled up in a puddle of moonlight, the sheet clutched around her, and tears on her cheeks. I freeze.

Oh shit. What happened? What did I do wrong?

I come up behind her and lie down, curling around her. "Hey," I purr in her ear. She un-balls slightly. "You're crying. Did I hurt you?"

"No," she mumbles, sniffling. "I'm just overwhelmed. I've never felt ... I mean, nobody's ever bothered ..."

"Sorry, what?" Confused, I brush her tangled hair aside and kiss the back of her neck. She's trembling, and the smell of sex rolls off her. If I hadn't just blown my load, I would be all over her.

"Sex wasn't ... like this. It was a chore, it was ... something I did *for* him." She's struggling for the words as I cradle her ... and suddenly I understand what she's saying.

Oh. Holy shit. I don't know whether to high-five myself for giving her her first orgasm or go back to the Nevada desert just to shoot Toby again.

"Your husband was a fool, a pig, and a shitty lover. You won't get any of that from me." I kiss her shoulder, and she starts to relax. "Promise."

We cuddle and doze for a while before she rises to shower and go sleep with her daughter. I know it's so Molly won't wake up calling for her again, but her absence nags at me as I pull on a pair of sleep shorts and crash again. I don't shower first. I like having her scent all over me.

When I wake up, it's daylight and they're still asleep. I quietly get up and grab the foot locker from the high shelf above the TV where I stashed it and open it up. Inside, a pair of untraceable .45s, two boxes of ammunition, and a burner phone sit on top of a bed of five hundred peso notes. After that weird feeling I got at the border crossing, I couldn't rest until I had armed myself again.

My gut tells me this isn't quite over yet.

I'm not in the mood for more burrito, so I get cleaned up and dressed and go downstairs to get some breakfast at the buffet. It's a nice, midrange resort—the kind families go to. The buffet offers a mix of local dishes and standard American tourist fare. Aside from my size, I don't look out of place wandering through in jeans to fill up my plate.

I notice a few people who, like me, stick slightly out among those clustered around the dozens of small tables. There's a towering young man having brunch with a tiny, sweet-faced older woman who beams at him as he tells her funny stories from his deployment. Mother or grandmother, I suspect. There's a statuesque, elegantly dressed woman with her hair pulled back tightly in a braid that goes halfway down her back. It's the lightest blonde I've ever seen.

There's a small, dark, neat man wearing an old-fashioned suit and spectacles, mildly eating an omelet, no meat on his plate. His hands are gloved, and he eats meticulously, knife and fork moving with surgical precision.

Nobody looks particularly threatening ... but I can feel the hairs on the back of my neck prickle again. I load up my plate with enough meat, eggs, and fruit to feed two bodybuilders. I fully intend to burn it all off in bed later today. Kids take afternoon naps, right?

I settle in at a corner table, watching the crowd as I eat. Still no sign of who might be setting off my alarm bells. Nobody's so much as looking my way, aside from a few curious glances.

Halfway through my meal, the little neat man quietly gets up and leaves, having finished his vegetarian breakfast.

I'm finishing my eggs when I look up and see the woman

with the white-blonde braid standing across the table from me. "Is this seat taken?" she asks quietly.

"I'm here with someone," I warn politely, not wanting to cause any misunderstandings.

She smiles. "No insult to your attractiveness, but that's not why I'm asking." She lifts an eyebrow and gestures toward the chair.

I nod and push it out with my foot. She sits primly, and I set down my fork. "So what's on your mind?"

"My name is Carolyn Moss. I'm here on business, Mr. Stone." Her voice is calm and nonthreatening, but her use of my real name immediately puts me on high alert. "Fortunately for you, I'm not from the Cohens. But they're here."

Ophelia. Molly. They're still not safe. "Then who are you with? The Milanos?"

"Good guess, but no." She takes a badge folder out of the inside of her dove-gray linen suit and my heart sinks. She slides it over without opening it. "Check it. You'll find it's legitimate."

I do. Special Agent Carolyn Moss, FBI. *Fuck.* "You're well out of your jurisdiction," I remind her flatly, and she nods.

"I'm not here to arrest you. I'm after someone bigger and nastier. They've sent a cleaner after you and your companions. Mr. Assante." She looks into my eyes with her cool, pale blue ones as all the blood drains from my face. "I see you've heard of him."

"Everyone who's anyone in Vegas has." Cleaners do more than remove evidence of crime scenes. They remove witnesses, and often any mobster who fucked up enough to require the cleaner in the first place. Mr. Assante is the Cohens' current top troubleshooter: a mystery man whose origin and appearance are unknown by almost everyone.

"Well, they know you're here, and they know your assumed name and those of the recently widowed Mrs. Whitman and her daughter. According to the communications that I intercepted, Assante has been sent for all three of you." She looks at me solemnly as I stare at her, breakfast forgotten.

"How did they find me?" *Where did I fuck up? Did I fuck up at all? Was it Ophelia or just bad luck?*

"They found out the assumed name you were using to check in, apparently. They also found out what border crossing you used. I suspect they used a computer expert to gather the information. Fortunately, that expert left a trail that one of my colleagues followed."

"Oh ..." *Shit.* "Why are you warning me?" I don't trust cops. They have always seemed more interested in hurting people than in protecting them.

"Why am I warning you, when you and I are the only ones in range to keep this man from murdering an innocent woman and a little girl?" Her gaze is unnervingly steady.

"You can't tell me you're just doing this out of idealism. Though, believe me, I'm grateful for the heads-up." *What the hell is her angle?*

"No, I'm not. Part of it is good old-fashioned self-serving ambition." She steeples her fingers.

I relax slightly. *So she wants some kind of deal.* "What do you mean?"

"Bringing in a rank-and-file hitter who wants out and is risking his neck to protect two civilians isn't that interesting to me. Bringing in an American Mafia legend with a body count in the hundreds, however ..." She smiles as her meaning dawns on me.

"You want Assante."

"That's right." Her eyes twinkle at my astonishment.

"And you want ... what from me? I can't turn state's evidence against him. I barely know anything about the guy." I glance around again, painfully aware that I don't have any idea what he looks like. Nobody does. Assante only ever associates with the Don himself.

"Oh, we have mountains of evidence against the man, thanks to an associate of mine." She doesn't elaborate. "I just want to grab him and get him back into the States where I can make the collar officially."

"So what part do I play? Bait?"

She smiles at me placidly.

"*Fuck*," I mutter under my breath. "Do you have any backup?"

"If I had backup, I wouldn't be asking for your help," she replies. "The San Diego office wouldn't have done much to help anyway, considering this is all happening in Mexico."

"What if I refuse you?" I'm wary of this ... and yet I may not have any choice but to play along. Taking on Assante alone, with Ophelia and that sweet little girl at risk, doesn't sound like a good idea at all.

"Then you take your chances that Assante will get to you before I can grab him." No mention of coming after me herself. Maybe she knows she can't top Assante in the terrifying department.

"Fine. Maybe we should share notes about Assante. Try and figure out who the hell he is before he can make his move." In the back of my head, I'm already planning an emergency call over to Jamie and his family, to get my boat over here as fast as possible.

Once Ophelia and Molly are safely aboard, Assante'll have a hell of a time getting to us. Even if he steals a boat and comes after us, I'll be able to see him coming.

"Aside from his many confirmed murders and the dozens he's suspected for, here's what I have gathered on him. He's in his fifties, is a master of multiple martial arts, and shows several of the diagnostic signs of being a sociopath." Her voice is all business and very calm, as if she's talking to a colleague.

She's not treating me like a criminal. It's actually refreshing. Kind of a maverick, this one. "Anything else?"

"He's very meticulous and a strict vegetarian. He's also apparently a germophobe." She sees my face and tilts her head. "Does that ring a bell with you?"

It does ... but it takes me a moment to realize why. When I do, I stand up at once. "Fuck."

"Stone. Talk to me." She gets up as well.

"He was sitting at that table over there, wearing gloves to eat breakfast. He was the only one in the room who didn't have meat on his plate. Right age, right manner, looked Sicilian." *Please let me be right. And let me be able to find the fucker again.*

"Then we had better find him before he locates your hotel room." We hurry out together while my mind races. I have to get to Ophelia and Molly—and my guns. I don't care if this cop gets the chance to bring in Assante alive, but he isn't laying a hand on that little girl—or on my woman.

We hurry up to my room—only to find the door unlocked. There are faint scratches around the keyhole that weren't there before. Someone's broken in. *Oh God.*

I shove the door open. "Ophelia!"

The answering silence tears at me. But there's no smell of cordite or blood, and as I race into the other room, I find it empty, too. One of the stuffed animals—Molly's worn-out favorite, the purple bear—is missing from the lineup on her bed, as obvious as a missing tooth. But she's nowhere to be found.

Calm down. Think. I stop dead, drawing a huge breath. *Did he kidnap them?*

"Stone, there's a note." Agent Moss' voice comes calmly from the other room, and I step out to check.

It's a note from Ophelia, left taped to the television. "'Taking a walk on the beach with Molly, be back in half an hour' ... shit. He'll have seen this."

"We need to get after them." She's checking her sidearm.

I go for the box in a hurry. It's a really bad idea to go after Assante unarmed. But when I flip it open, all I can do is stare at the contents.

The guns are missing.

"Do you think Assante has a firearm?" Moss asks as she holsters her own.

"He does now," I mutter in breathless horror—then turn to run out the door.

12

CHAPTER 12

O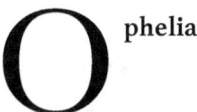phelia

"You're smiling a lot, Mommy. It's nice." Molly beams up at me as I hold her hand. Our footprints trail behind us in the wet sand at the sea's edge—a morning walk before breakfast.

It's still a little chilly with a gray layer of cloud on the horizon and the sky a pale blue. The waves are choppy from the wind, which blows my olive-green gauze skirt against my legs as we walk.

"I have reasons to smile," I reply in a light voice. Some of the reasons, I can even tell her: we're away from her daddy, we're safe, nobody's going to hurt us like that again. It hurts my heart that she understands, at such a young age, that her father was a terrible person—someone to be afraid of.

Then there's the one big reason I can't tell her about—at least not until she's a whole lot older. I learned a whole new dimension of sex last night, from climaxing to being held afterward. I couldn't fully explain to Brian why I was weeping then, but now I understand the deep sadness that hit as I realized what I had put up with in the place of real lovemaking for too many years.

"Are we gonna stay with Brian from now on?" Molly asks, sounding eager at the prospect. "I like him. He's much nicer than Daddy."

Holy crap, sweetheart. "I want you to know that if I could have, I would have taken you and left Daddy a long time ago. Brian helped." *And I'm not telling you the full story about that for years either.*

I helped kill my husband. I can think that now without shame. I helped kill my husband, but he was a monster, and his bosses were monsters. And there was no stopping a man like that. A man who had the Mob at his disposal to chase me down and deliver me back to him if I tried to run. *No stopping him without a goddamn bullet, that is.*

"So we're staying with him? On the island?" She hops along beside me and then stops short to inspect something in the sand that's spitting out a stream of water.

I stop with her. "I'm sure thinking about it. Anyway, we have a whole month to stay here and decide."

"Okay. But I vote we keep him." She skips ahead and back again and then squats to poke at the hole in the sand. "What is this?"

"That's a clam, honey. They get sand stuck in their shells and spit out a bunch of water to clean themselves out." I heel-sit next to her, gathering my skirt in one hand to keep it from trailing in the wet sand.

"Why do they live in the sand if they don't want it in their shells?" She tilts her head and then pokes at the hole again. Another bit of water spurts out, and she snatches her hand back with an "Eek!"

"So the birds won't pry open their shells and eat them." How long has it been since I had an innocent moment together with my daughter, just teaching her things and being a mom? Too long. I'm really glad to be able to do it again.

And none of it would have been possible without Brian. Whom I'm falling for hard, if I'm not already there. And the way he acts ... I think he feels the same.

What a wonderful morning.

"We should go back and have our burritos soon," I start, only to hear a faint call from behind us.

I turn to look, hoping it's Brian. But it's an older man I don't recognize, striding energetically down the beach after us with something floppy and purple in his hand. He's dark-haired, graying, and wears spectacles and gloves. He smiles mildly as he holds up the object.

"Hello!" he calls as he draws nearer. "I'm very sorry, but your daughter seems to have dropped this."

"My bear!" Molly straightens up and beams—then bolts toward the man, hands out. "Oh, thank you! I guess I forgot him!"

Wait.

Maybe it's the time I've spent with Brian. Maybe it's being married to the fucking mob for years. But my natural wariness kicks in—and I make a grab for my daughter's arm a moment before the reason registers: she didn't bring the bear with us when we left the hotel room. How and why does he even have it?

She stops short and blinks up at me. "But, Mommy, my bear!"

"It's okay, honey. Just give me a second." I look up at the man, whose eyes behind his spectacles are a gentle chocolate brown ... except the smile on his lips doesn't reach them. "Who are you?"

He sighs in exasperation and tosses the bear aside into the sand. I see the pistol in his hand and my blood turns to ice water.

"My name is Assante. You won't have heard of me. Your connection to my employer is entirely incidental, after all."

He's from the Cohens. Oh God. Brian ... where are you? You said you'd keep us safe!

"You're in clear view of the resort. There will be witnesses. You can't just—" I freeze as he holds up his free hand imperiously.

"I suppose there will be, but by the time anyone manages to get close enough to identify us, I'll be gone. Believe me, young lady, I've been doing this job longer than you've been alive." His smile quirks slightly, sending a wave of terror and nausea through me.

I shove Molly behind me, looking around frantically. No cover. We could run into the water, but he would just shoot us in the back.

"I am very sorry about this, really. If anything, Mr. Stone is to blame. He knows better than to leave witnesses behind." His voice is almost serene as his finger slips into the trigger guard.

"Mommy?" my baby cries out in fear. I hug her tight and cover her eyes with my hand, trying to shield her with my body. There's nowhere to go, and nothing to do but pray that it's quick.

But before Assante can pull the trigger, I hear a bellow of outrage that could have come from an angry bull. The man with the gun turns his head—and his eyes widen slightly in concern before he turns quickly and shifts targets to a furious, charging Brian.

"Molly, get down!" I cry as I lunge forward and shove the man's gun arm to the side. The gun goes off. Brian grunts in pain and grabs his side but doesn't even break stride.

The man turns to backhand me with surprising strength, knocking me straight to the sand. I land next to Molly, ears ringing, but before he can turn his attention to Brian, there's a bone-jarring thud and a grunt of pain. The pistol goes flying past me and lands in the shallows with a plop.

I raise my head to see Brian squaring off with the man, whose eyes narrow with amusement. "You're bleeding," he notes as Brian draws a bloody fist away from his side.

"Yeah, I am," Brian growls, face white with fury. "I'm still gonna kick your ass."

I look up the hill at the resort; there are a few people up there, but all but one are running away from the confrontation, not toward it. The one who isn't—an elegant-looking woman with a light blonde braid—is running straight for us with a pistol held down at her side.

"I don't know how you plan to do that," the man replies mildly as he pulls another gun from under his suit coat. "Seeing as I am armed, and you are not—"

I've never seen anyone Brian's size move that fast. All I see is him turn around while lifting his leg—and then there's a thwack and the second pistol goes spinning away while Assante clutches an obviously broken gun hand.

"Like that, fucker," Brian snarls as he lunges for the man.

CHAPTER 13

Brian

I'VE NEVER RUN SO FAST in my entire goddamned life. I bolt down to the beach, startling passersby, scaring birds into the air, and leaving my muscles and lungs burning. The beach is almost deserted; I catch sight of footprints padding along the tide line. Two barefoot—medium and tiny—and one in wingtip shoes.

He's after them. He's already on their heels. I ignore the pain and push even harder.

Agent Moss trails behind but doesn't call after me to slow down. I wouldn't listen even if she did. Then I see the figures in the distance—and everything starts to go very fast.

I don't feel the bullet scoring my side when Assante fires. I don't hesitate for a moment when he pulls out the other .45. There's nothing to do but keep attacking until Assante either kills me or Moss catches up and gets her gun on him.

"Well played. But I can still kill all three of you before

anyone comes to help." The son of a bitch wants banter with his combat on top of everything else.

I don't oblige, unleashing a flurry of blows instead, trying to drive him away from Ophelia and Molly—and from where the gun has dropped. I can't trust that the wet sand has fouled it.

Now that he knows I'm competent, he's not playing around anymore, moving so fluidly that I can't land a single punch or kick. I press forward anyway, feeling my side get stickier and wetter, feeling the creaky pain in my ribs, but knowing I have to keep him on the defensive.

"Goodness me, you're certainly putting your everything into this," he comments, still maddeningly calm. "One would think you had something to save on this beach besides your own life."

I jab fast to keep him at a distance. He leans out of the way and gets in under my guard briefly, grabbing my arm and locking it up. I lean with his movement before he can break the bone; his wounded hand loses its grip and I drive my free elbow back into his face.

His glasses shatter and he stumbles backward, blood seeping through his fingers as he grabs his face. I try to get in another blow, but then he tears away the bloody glasses and blocks unerringly, even half blinded.

"Are you telling me that you betrayed your oath to us and ran for it because of a woman you just barely met?" He tuts at me as he ducks another blow. "So unprofessional. There's a reason why romantics are called hopeless."

The blood loss is starting to make me lightheaded—but I'm still on my feet, and he's wounded, too. "You only mock love because you can't feel it, you numb prick." I'm surprised when genuine anger blooms across his bleeding face.

"Only a fool is proud of his weaknesses!" I barely dodge his snap-kick under my chin; he presses the attack, focused only on me now, confusing me with the cold fury on his face. "And now you've gotten your filthy blood on me!"

Oh right. A germophobe. "You shot me and now you're bitching at me for bleeding? Really?" I can't afford to look over my shoulder to see how far up the beach Moss has gotten. Assante is genuinely fighting now, the blows coming fast, hard, and almost impossible to dodge.

"Disgusting. I'll need a course of antibiotics after this. But first I'll crush your throat." And he stabs two fingers at me so fast, I can barely move in time to keep them from striking me in the larynx.

I dodge, then spit in his face.

He stumbles back, frantically wiping at his face, his goal of murdering me forgotten for a moment. And in that one split second, I follow the gob of spit with a fist.

I hit him so hard, my knuckle-skin splits with flashes of fresh pain. He goes flying backward into the sand and lands there, dazed. "You filthy, cheating wretch—" he starts a second before I kick him in the face and watch a couple of his teeth fly. The back of his head hits the sand, and he blinks up at the sky, as if shocked that my desperate, dirty-fighting ass actually beat him.

But that's the thing about master martial artists. The opponent they fear isn't another master. It's some desperate rando with no sportsmanship, no way to predict his moves, and everything to lose.

"Brian!" Ophelia is on her feet, and bless her, she has the gun. She runs to me, then hugs me carefully. I hug back one-armed as Molly clamps onto my leg, crying.

"It's okay, ladies. It's over. He can't hurt you anymore." And if he tries, I will crush his fucking skull.

"You know," Assante says mildly, "others will come once I tell them where you are."

"Oh, we won't be here by the time anyone else arrives." I

smile despite my pain. "Besides, do you really think any one of them is gonna want to try taking down the man who kicked *your* ass?"

He doesn't have any answer for that and sulkily looks away.

A moment later, Moss runs up, aiming her own pistol at Assante. Ophelia blinks at the sudden arrival. "Who are you?"

"Carolyn Moss, FBI. I'm after this murdering bastard here." She keeps the gun pointed at Assante. "Don't even think about moving," she tells him.

"That ... would be difficult at this juncture," he says, sighing and holding obligingly still. "But aren't you out of your jurisdiction?"

"Maybe. But nobody's gonna believe you when you tell them that," I inform Assante. The adrenaline is beginning to wear off and my ribs really start to hurt. I turn to the agent. "You got any handcuffs?"

"Nope," she responds with surprising amusement. She hands me her gun. "Keep this on him. I have something better."

When she pulls out the roll of duct tape, Assante's eyes widen in outrage. I grin as I hold the trembling Ophelia close.

"Make a duct tape mummy!" Molly demands from behind my leg. "He kidnapped my bear and scared everybody!"

"Now that is just excessive—" Assante protests. "My suit—"

Smiling widely, Agent Moss rips off the first length of duct tape. "I'll do my best," she promises Molly.

Then she plasters the tape right over his mouth.

CHAPTER 14

phelia

BRIAN DOESN'T GET out of the hospital until late that afternoon. They can't do much for cracked ribs, but they stitch up the gash in his side and give him antibiotics and painkillers. Between that and the beating he took from Assante, he's sore and a touch grumpy by the time we walk out to the car.

I'm doing better, but Molly's wiped out, napping on my shoulder as she clings to my front like a baby koala. I keep my arms tight around her, unwilling to let her go again.

"Are you angry at me?" he asks. "I almost couldn't keep my promise."

"No. The only guys to blame are the Cohens and that Assante bastard. Did that FBI agent actually drive him to the hospital while duct taped like that? I can't imagine her being so kind, but then again, I'm ready to kill the bastard myself for pointing a gun at my daughter."

"He never arrived at the hospital, according to the police who talked to me. They don't know about Agent Moss, which is probably good." He settles into the driver's seat, grunting softly at the discomfort from his side.

"You don't think he killed her and escaped?" I worry aloud.

He laughs. "Nope. I think he's going back to America in the trunk of her rental car."

I remember the look of outrage on Assante's face as Agent Moss duct taped his bloody mouth shut. "Couldn't have happened to a nicer guy."

"I don't know what we would have done if she hadn't shown up," Brian admits as I get Molly settled in the back and buckle her seat belt. "Seems weird. Almost like someone other than the FBI sent her."

"I think you're selling yourself short. All she did was give the warning. You took that man down on your own. But it *is* a little weird. Do you have any secret agent friends?" I ask as I shut Molly's door and slip into my own.

"Not that I know of. But her help was ... essential. And if I didn't know it's probably all just coincidence, I would believe that's why she was sent."

"Almost enough to make you rethink your feelings about law enforcement all being bastards, huh?" I buckle my seat belt.

He chuckles and nods as he starts the car. "Anyway, I owe her one. I hope her star rises fast when she delivers that prick to the Bureau."

"Me, too. But anyway, enough about them. I'm starved and my feet hurt. Let's go back to the hotel. You said your friend Jamie and his family are meeting us for dinner?"

"Yeah. They're bringing my boat. We can have a barbecue on deck. His daughter's about Molly's age. You think she'll be up for it?" He sounds concerned, and I smile.

"She'll be okay once I wash and stitch up her bear. She's a

tough kid. Maybe tougher than me."

Molly opens an eye. "Nobody better hurt my bear again."

"No, they'd better not, or I'll beat them up, too. Promise." Brian seems as stunned as I am about how resilient Molly has turned out to be. We'll have to watch her after this, of course; all this misadventure has to have left a mark. But despite that, I think she's going to be okay.

"Good. You can beat up bad guys, like Batman," Molly says.

He laughs, not sounding too bothered by the comparison. "I'm not rich enough to be Batman. But I'll try."

"So when are we going to the island?" Molly punctuates her question with a yawn and blinks slowly. "I wanna go."

Brian and I exchange warm glances. He wants me with him on that island, for good. Molly, too. I have mixed feelings about it. Molly will need an education, and I'm not sure I can do that all on my own. But for now ... an idyllic hideaway on the warm Pacific sounds almost perfect.

"We can't move in until the house is built," Brian says firmly. "That's why a month. But we can go visit this weekend, if you want."

"We're going on a boat? Yay!" She bounces in her seat delightedly against the seat belt.

"Yeah." Brian smiles as he focuses on the road. "And then a secret island. It'll be neat."

"Can I bring all my stuffies?" Of course, the most important of questions from my sweet daughter. And her asking makes it even more clear: she's going to be okay.

And as long as the three of us are together ... so am I.

I'm smiling as we make our way back to the hotel for a well-deserved rest. It may be a bit before Brian is healed up enough to make love to me again ... but that's all right.

Thanks to him, we have plenty of time.

The End.

EPILOGUE

Carolyn

"So you get sent after Stone, chase him to San Diego, and then come back with Geraldo Assante instead?" Daniels sounds absolutely stunned. "He's actually in the lockup under federal guard right now? How the hell did you pull that off?"

"I found out that Stone was trying to defect. The Cohens usually use Assante to sanction any hitters who go astray, so when it came down to choosing who to chase, I picked the man we have the much stronger case against." There's so much more to it than that, but Daniels doesn't need to know all the details.

Those, I'm saving for Prometheus.

"We've been trying to catch that son of a bitch for fifteen years, and you just happen to stumble across him in the field. For fuck's sake." He leans back in his desk chair, laughing incredulously.

I keep my smile frozen on my face, my fists clenching and unclenching behind my back. "Opportunities like that don't knock very often, sir."

"No, I guess they don't." He eyes me, a mild glint of suspicion in them. "Still ... you have had an awful lot of good luck lately."

"Good luck comes with good leads, sir. The rest was hard work." He doesn't need to know that ninety percent of my "good leads" don't come from him.

"Well, I can't say I don't work you hard." He sounds grudging. Daniels' return to work is very conditional, if the rumors are correct, but here he is at his desk anyway, pretending like nothing's happened.

I know the truth. Your wife is gone, your reputation is rapidly heading into the toilet, your job's in jeopardy, and the female agent who you tried to punish with a series of impossible jobs is kicking ass instead.

Daniels' star is falling while mine rises, and I know who to thank for both.

But the question remains: why is Prometheus helping me?

"Assante claims that you chased him into Mexico, kidnapped him, and smuggled him back into the States in the trunk of your car, like a damn mobster." He's taking notes with a pen as we talk. "There's no evidence of that, though he was injured. Do you have anything to say about that?"

"I think Geraldo Assante will say anything to try and get his case thrown out."

I also think that duct taping him and stuffing him in my trunk was uniquely satisfying. So were all those detours along rocky, winding Mexican back roads on the way home.

"Well, we have dozens of witnesses against him. We really don't need any more testimony. Even if this arrest gets thrown out, we can turn around and rearrest him for fifty other things."

He sniffs. "I'd put you up for a commendation, but I don't want this going to your head."

Well, fuck you too, then. But I'll still get credit for the collar. "Is that all, sir?" I ask almost gently.

He grunts and waves a hand. "Yeah, time to move on to number four on your list. I'll have the file and plane tickets to Detroit out to you by tomorrow morning. Flight's that afternoon." He flicks his hand again, as if dismissing a servant. "Get moving."

"Yes, sir," I reply as I turn to leave, fighting the urge to laugh.

Back in my car, I glance around, then pull out the phone Prometheus gave me and text him.

Daniels is back and getting suspicious. He's sending me on another case tomorrow. No commendation. I think he's trying to figure out how to take credit for my collar.

The answer comes in a few minutes.

He will find that difficult. Interesting that he was able to avoid any serious disciplinary action. He must have connections within the Bureau that I'm not aware of.

"Or the devil's own luck," I grumble. But that's all right. I can make my own luck—especially with the right kind of help.

I wanted to thank you. You've done a great deal to help me.

His answer surprises me.

All I did was offer the information. You chose to listen and act on it. I am glad to have found you. It is rare to find someone whose ethics match her ambitions.

Get some rest, Carolyn. I will contact you when you get to Detroit.

"How did he know I'm going to—" I start, but there's no point writing to ask him. I know that as with many things, Prometheus isn't about to spill his secrets.

But one day, I'm going to track him down and get answers to

all of them. I don't know what that meeting will be like, but I already know that I'm not going to stop until I find him.

T̲ʜᴇ E̲ɴᴅ.

SIGN UP TO RECEIVE FREE BOOKS

Sign Up to Receive Free E-Books and Audiobook Codes.

WOULD you like to read **Savage Hearts** and **other romance books** for **free**?

YOU CAN SIGN up to receive free e-books and audiobooks by typing this link into your browser:

HTTPS://IVYWONDERSAUTHOR.COM/IVY-WONDERS-AUTHOR

©Copyright 2020 by Ivy Wonder All rights Reserved
In no way is it legal to reproduce, duplicate, or transmit any part of this document in either electronic means or in printed format. Recording of this publication is strictly prohibited and any storage of this document is not allowed unless with written permission from the publisher. All rights are reserved.
Respective authors own all copyrights not held by the publisher.

Created with Vellum

www.ingramcontent.com/pod-product-compliance
Lightning Source LLC
LaVergne TN
LVHW011723060526
838200LV00051B/3001